OFF COURSE

A SINS OF THE MAFIA WORLD NOVEL

SCARRED HEROES BOOK 2

GWYN MCNAMEE

PROLOGUE

CHAOS

The perfectly still, quiet, dark night, lit only by the millions of stars and the partially cloud-obscured moon, shatters in an instant.

A planned cataclysm.

Deliberate devastation.

Total assured destruction.

Methodical chaos.

The well-executed explosion rips through the dilapidated building, sending handmade mudbricks and mortar flying skyward and out in a tidal wave of debris. Bits and pieces of the structure plunge to the ground like rain from the heavens, but unlike the water this desert so desperately needs, it doesn't quench a desperate thirst and feed life into the crops and animals; the stuff falling from the sky will kill you with its force.

If I've done my job, there won't be anyone alive in there to feel the rubble striking them, though.

And I always do my job well.

I used enough C4 to destroy a building twice that size. Some might argue I overdid it. That using more than necessary wastes resources. Some might say it's overkill. But when it comes to eliminating a threat, I always go all-out.

It's the one thing I'm good at. The one thing the guys can always count on. They call me in when they need chaos, and I bring it. I ensure the enemy is nothing but dust in the desert wind.

Reaper watches the fallout through his night vision goggles next to me, silently assessing every inch of visible real estate in front of us. The village remains still despite the blast.

Smoke billows high into the night sky, flames leaping up and dancing merrily as if in celebration of my achievement. Even after all these years and countless missions, it never gets old seeing the orangey-red glow of my success.

Only, the internal celebration is short-lived.

An eerie silence falls over the small desert village just rocked by my hand. A slow, cold tingle spreads through my body, sending the hairs on the back of my neck up and putting me on high alert.

Something's wrong.

I don't even have time to call out a warning before gunfire tears through the smoky night air and slams into me.

Fuck.

Pain explodes through my side, and I roll to my left toward Reaper just in time to avoid another fusillade of bullets hitting where I was just lying. "Where the hell is that coming from?"

Reaper scans the village and focuses to the right and up. "Three o'clock."

I wince and press my hand against my side. Warm blood seeps between my fingers, a bullet having hit one of the spots not covered by my body armor. I pull off my night vision goggles and examine the wound as best I can. "Where the hell is Mouth?"

"I'm here, guys. Repositioning," Mouth's voice comes through our com.

Reaper peers over at me. "Are you hit?"

I try to take a deep breath but end up coughing—whether it's from the smoke in the air or because the bullet hit something vital remains to be seen. "I'm fine."

"That doesn't answer my question. Were you fucking hit?"

"I'm *fine*." I barely manage to grind out the words through clenched teeth as we wait for Mouth to do his thing.

Without him to provide cover, we'll be trapped here, sitting ducks for whoever managed to escape the explosion and now seems intent on ensuring we don't make it out of this hellhole alive.

I watch the building at our three o'clock for any signs of movement. Whoever was shooting has momentarily stopped, but they're likely just reloading or adjusting positions. "How the fuck did anyone get out?"

When we scouted the village, almost all the residents had fled, leaving it in the control of the insurgents we're here for, and those fuckers had chosen a central location within the small cluster of buildings to act as their headquarters. It was our primary target, and given everything we'd seen during our recon, they all should have been there and long asleep before it blew.

One calculated strike to remove a pesky problem for the forces in the area—or, at least, it should have been.

Reaper shrugs as he surveys the village. "Who the fuck knows, with these guys. Might not even be one of them. Might be some villager who didn't get the fuck out in time who picked up a weapon they found lying on the damn street."

"Ready to light 'em up, if you are, motherfuckers." Mouth's cheery sing-song voice cuts through the com.

Having him up there doesn't mean we're safe down here, but it's better than the alternative—trying to get back to the exfil spot with someone trying to peg us off.

I push myself up slightly to check the building where we last saw the threat, clouded in smoke from my explosion. "You have the shooter?"

"Movement in the north window. He's either reloading or jerking off."

Reaper's gaze shifts up, trying to see what Mouth can from his position. "Do you have the shot?"

"Negative."

I scan the town square in front of us, searching for the rest of the unit. "Where are Mayhem and Flash?"

Mayhem's voice cuts through the com. "Coming up on your six."

Flash and Mayhem make their way over to us, moving silently through the outskirts of the village, eyes on the building containing the shooter.

Mayhem settles next to me. "We had to circle around to avoid the town square."

"Any resistance on your side of town?"

He shakes his head. "Nah. We saw your handiwork but not a living soul."

Where the fuck did this shooter come from?

It's like he just popped up out of nowhere—a ghost with an assault rifle and a hard-on for killing American troops.

Flash takes position next to Reaper and inclines his head toward the east, where the rising sun will break the horizon in only a couple of hours. "We need to get the fuck out of here and to exfil. Mouth?"

"Still no shot."

Reaper glances to where Mouth is perched atop the roof of another mudbrick building, waiting for his opportunity to pick off the shooter so he doesn't use us for target practice when we try to make it to where the helo will pick us up. "We're gonna have to draw that fucker out." He points to me. "Chaos stays here.

Mayhem, you're with me. Flash...do your thing. He's gonna have to choose a target and should bring himself into Mouth's sights."

Reaper, Mayhem, and Flash head out in the respective directions—each keeping to the darkest of the shadows until the exact right time when Flash's speed comes into play.

The man moves faster than a damn lightning bolt and has managed to outrun any bullet that's ever been fired at him. He will again tonight. With Reaper, Mayhem, and me providing cover, Flash will draw the shooter to the window where Mouth can end this.

I shift into a better position, sharp pain slicing at my side. My vision blurs slightly, the smoke and darkness of the night creeping in at the edges, but I shake my head and force my eyes open.

Gunfire erupts from my three o'clock. Reaper and Mayhem both return fire. The wind kicks up, pushing more smoke lingering from the explosion through the town square, further obscuring the view for anyone without the benefit of night vision.

The crunch of footsteps behind me makes me whirl in that direction, weapon ready. A tall lone figure approaches in the faint moonlight, holding something long pointed in my direction.

I fire, and he cries out and stumbles forward, then drops to the sand.

Almost instantly, a blast from behind me, in the center of town, propels me forward. The rock-hard ground knocks the air from my lungs, and I struggle to keep the world around me in focus, blinking rapidly to clear the bright spots from my vision.

The night sky erupts with a towering blaze and more smoke that's sure to draw in others from the surrounding mountains. We won't be alone here for long.

I focus on the body on the ground ten yards in front of me. A form huddles over it. Another figure. Someone who wasn't there only moments ago.

Wailing carries through the night.

A woman.

Pieces of her words reach me.

Broken but enough for me to translate.

My son!

I stagger to my feet as Reaper's voice comes through the com.

"Mayhem is down. I have him. They just shot a damn rocket into the fucking building where Mouth was set up."

His words register slowly, like my brain has been soaked in high-octane bourbon.

"Mouth? Mouth?" Flash's breathing comes ragged and heavy, like he's running hard again. "I'm going in after him, but we have company. We're going to be shooting our way out of here."

The woman in front of me finally seems to sense I'm there and turns toward me. She cries out, reaching for whatever her son had in his hand.

Metal glints in the moonlight.

Gun.

"Where the hell is Chaos?"

I cough and try to respond to Reaper as I struggle to bring up my weapon with weak arms. It's like being under water. Drowning and not being able to see the surface. Every breath filling my lungs with fluid. She aims the weapon in my direction, stepping closer through the smoke.

Somehow, I manage to fire off a single shot, the sound sharp and final.

She crumples to the ground next to her son, the gun in her hand clattering to the hard, compacted earth. I drop to my knees, my legs no longer able to support my weight. My breaths come ragged. Wheezing and wet.

The world darkens...

Shit.

Avery is going to be fucking pissed.

1

FOUR YEARS LATER

AVERY

I jerk the wheel to the right to avoid the car I didn't even notice was in front of me in my lane. My phone tumbles from my center console and onto the floor on the passenger side. A horn blares, and the man driving the car I almost just side-swiped to avoid hitting the *other* car flips me off.

Fuck.

The world blurs, my hot tears making it virtually impossible to see the road or anything else. I wipe at my eyes, trying to clear my vision, but it doesn't help.

Just get home.

Just get home where you can think and figure out what to do.

You just need to think.

I keep telling myself that, repeating it *ad nauseum* the entire drive, somehow hoping the more I say it, the more I'll believe it and the greater the chance it might be true. It's wishful thinking at its finest, but it's all I have left to cling to after what I just saw.

My hands won't stop shaking, though, because deep down, I know it won't be okay. Getting home won't help anything. I'll still be in the same damn position, just sobbing on my couch instead of in my car, seeing the same thing over and over again in my head, reliving it every waking moment and refusing to sleep so it doesn't visit me there, too.

It's a mistake.

It has to be.

Another lie I keep telling myself—one I want so badly to believe because the alternative—that I *really* saw what I did, that it really means what I think it does—is just too horrific to accept.

But I know what I saw.

I just want to pretend this was all some bad dream, some hallucination, some sort of warping of my mind brought on by the time of year and the turmoil it always dredges up from the past.

It's just an awake nightmare brought on by stress, nothing more.

Yeah, keep telling yourself that, Avery.

I quickly swipe the tears from my eyes to try to clear my sight again and suck in a deep breath, but concentrating on what's happening outside this car, outside the vivid visions playing in my head, becomes harder and harder.

How could I have been so stupid?

So blind?

So trusting?

I've always prided myself on my ability to see through bullshit. To see people's true intentions, deep into their souls. Or at least, I did. Before Kalen. Combined with what just happened, it's abundantly clear that my radar is so far out of whack that it can't ever be fixed. I'm apparently a very shitty judge of character, and now, my failure has gotten me into this mess.

What I thought was a green light at the upcoming intersection flips to red, and I slam on my brakes and skid to a screeching stop, barely avoiding careening into the intersection and cross traffic.

Holy hell.

My heart thunders against my ribcage, and I press my hand over it, sucking in short gasps of air that seem to do nothing to help clear my head or fill my lungs.

How did I miss that turning yellow?

That's twice now, in the last five minutes, I almost killed myself because I can't see straight enough to drive. I'm supposed to be getting *away* from danger, not driving myself right into it.

Get a grip.

If I don't, I'm going to end up dead on this damn road and none of this will matter, anyway.

Traffic flows past in front of me, the good people of Baltimore making their way home after a late dinner or a long day at the office.

It's the time of night that bad things happen.

I should have known better than to be there.

Vivid, fresh memories flash before my eyes, the very thing I'm running from refusing to give me quarter for even a moment, and I squeeze them closed for a minute, hoping to will away what I saw with that simple action.

It doesn't work.

I reopen them, and the darkness of the night makes my skin crawl. Even with the headlights, the street-lights, and the buzz of movement surrounding me, there are too many shadows. Too many unknowns. Anything can be hiding out there. Anyone...

It's something I've never really thought about before, how truly vulnerable we all are at any given time, likely because I always had Kalen looking out for me, protecting me and making me feel safe...until he didn't. But now, I can't shake the feeling of eyes on me, of someone or something watching and waiting for the opportunity to strike.

With the light still red, I lean over and try to reach around the floor well on the passenger side for my phone. My fingers brush hard plastic, and I scoop it up and glance down at the screen.

Shit.

The little one percent on the battery indicator taunts me, red and glowing, the same color as the blood I can't get out of my visions.

So much blood...

I sit back up and settle into my seat, dropping my phone into the cup holder again. Almost instantly, blinding headlights hit my rearview mirror. A large SUV or truck barrels down at me from behind. Still half a block away, it doesn't appear to be slowing down as it approaches rapidly, ready to ram into my car and send me out into the cross traffic.

Shit. They're going to hit me.

The traffic light remains red, and traffic whizzes in front of me, a river of cars I can't make my way across. If this asshole doesn't stop, there's nowhere to go except into the middle of the intersection to be T-boned.

I throw my wheel to the right and floor it, hoping to squeeze between the curb and the oncoming traffic just as the SUV clips the back of my car. It sends me careening sideways into the fray. My side of the car slams into something, whipping my head to the left. I lay on my brakes, and the SUV that hit me continues straight into the intersection, smashing into a large truck with a sickening bang and crunch.

Gasping, my brain fogged and heart beating a rapid tattoo, I fumble to put my car into park and turn my head to observe the disaster behind me. The SUV that struck me sits in the middle of the intersection, its entire front end collapsed against the passenger side of a sedan that was also rear-ended by another car. Smoke rises from both vehicles, obscuring my view.

Shit.

Is everyone okay?

I reach for my seatbelt but pause with my hand on it as the passenger door of the SUV swings open and a familiar figure steps out on the pavement which is littered with shards of glass and pieces of metal that have been violently torn from the various vehicles involved.

"Oh, my God..." My stomach turns, the acid threatening to make its way up my throat. "No!"

I crank the gearshift, trying to get it into drive, and the back window just behind my head explodes, glass flying everywhere, hitting the side of my face. Sharp bites of pain aren't enough to stop me from understanding what just happened.

He's shooting *at me!*

Another shot pings against the door, and I slam my foot against the gas, but nothing happens. The engine revs violently, but I don't move—frozen in place, watching the man advance, still shooting.

I fumble with the gear again, finally getting it to move from neutral to drive as two more bullets strike the car.

Fuck.

I floor the gas, and this time, the vehicle complies, barreling away from the curb, leaving the accident, other angry drivers, and the apparent death squad sent after me, behind.

Sobs tumble from my lips, and the tears come so fast, there's no way to stop them even if I wanted to try.

What the hell am I going to do?

Not go home.

If I do, they'll show up eventually—likely quickly if

they were concerned enough to send *that* man after me so fast tonight.

They know I know.

They know I saw.

They can't let me live with the information I have.

I reach a shaking hand for my phone. "You know what you need to do."

My own voice mixing with the noises of the street and the city outside coming into the car from the broken window helps me develop some clarity.

"There's only one person you can call, Avery."

I can't. I can't. I can't.

I glance in my rearview mirror to see if anyone else is following me, the accident now so far behind me that I can't even see it anymore. The road remains empty, the traffic blocked by the cataclysm at the intersection.

"You don't have a choice."

It's the same thing I told myself all those years ago, that I didn't have a choice, that he was *forcing* me to make the decision I had to that changed so much.

I open the phone and dial the number I still know by heart, the one he said to only use in emergencies, one I hope he still answers. It's been so long that it's likely disconnected by now, all ties cut the same way he slashed everything and everyone else out of his life.

Still, I have to try.

It doesn't even ring before the familiar recorded voice hits my ear. "*Leave it.*"

Hearing him after so long draws a violent sob from

deep in my chest. I swallow past the rock lodged in my throat and try to blink away the rapidly falling tears so I don't end up crashing into something else. "Kalen, I'm in trouble. I don't know what to do. I need you—"

My phone issues a sharp beep in my hand, and I pull it away from my ear and glance down at a black screen.

"No! No! No!"

It's dead.

And so am I.

***

CHAOS

MY FIST CONNECTS with the hard jawbone of the motherfucker strapped to the chair in front of me, the force vibrating up through my arm in a satisfying sting as his head snaps back.

This fucker deserves so much worse.

He recovers from the blow, slowly shaking his head to try to clear the stars he's no doubt seeing after the way I've been working him over the last few minutes.

I squat, resting my forearms on my knees and watching the blood trickle from the corner of his mouth and nose. "I told you you didn't want to mess with her again, didn't I? I gave you a fair warning, and what did you do? Not even two weeks after we had our last chat, you thought showing up at her work was going to fly?"

A strangled groan slips from his lips, but I can't tell if it was meant to be a word or just a reaction to the agony he must be in. Hopefully, the latter. He's hanging just at that edge of blacking out, but that would be too good for him, too easy.

I won't let that happen.

Not until my job is done.

I reach forward and grasp his hair, forcing his head up until his unfocused muddy-brown eyes meet mine. "You really thought I wouldn't be there? Watching her? Protecting her? Making sure your punk ass didn't show up to cause more trouble?" I bark out a laugh that echoes in the empty, dilapidated boathouse. "You are one dumb fucker, aren't you? You just couldn't stay away."

My chest tightens slightly, knowing how hard that can be, and I push up to my full height, release his hair, and cross my arms over my chest.

The moment Robyn showed up at the office, asking for protection, and told us the history with this douchebag, I had a feeling it wouldn't be quick to resolve. Unlike a lot of our jobs—get in, get out, leave nothing but bodies behind—obsession is a whole other animal.

It twists the mind. Makes people irrational. Causes them to act against their own best interests. Makes them forget completely about self-preservation.

And Ryan Andrew Long is one obsessed man.

That creepy shrine to Robyn in his houseboat was all the proof I needed to know he wouldn't stop even after the first warning, which is why I never took my eyes off her and caught him tonight in the one place he should have stayed miles away from.

It's why he's suffering now.

Why he *deserves* to suffer.

Still, killing him is off the table for a variety of reasons. Robyn would know. The police could become involved and dig due to the restraining order she has against him, and she isn't trained to hold up under questioning. The firm's name would fall from her lips, and they'd end up on the doorstep with a warrant and questions we can't answer—at least, not without going to prison for a *very, very* long time.

Since my favorite permanent way to ensure our clients remain safe isn't available, that means coming up with new, creative strategies.

I scan the old boathouse that clearly hasn't been used in years. The half-crumbled roof lies in pieces on the broken concrete floor. Rats scurry in the shadows. The water of the Patapsco River laps against the moorings in the empty boat slip. Combined with the moonlight streaming in from the holes in the roof, it provides the perfect ambiance for what I have to do.

Squatting again, I wait until Ryan lifts his head to meet my gaze. "Do you have a favorite movie, Ryan?"

"Wh-what?"

I raise an eyebrow. "Do you have a favorite movie?"

"Wh-why? I don't—"

"Because I'm about to make a point here, Ryan. Let me tell you about *my* favorite movie." I examine the blood on my knuckles and smile. "*Casino Royale.*" Looking back at him, I wait for the connection to click in his head, but he remains almost passive, his face gaunt and pale, the blood still falling to the concrete below him from various places. "Have you not seen it?"

He shakes his head slightly. "No...I mean...yes...a l-long time a-ago."

"Well, it's absolutely *brilliant.* Not only did it launch Daniel Craig as the new Bond, but it also has one of my favorite movie scenes of all time—where Bond is tortured by *Le Chiffre.*"

I let the words hang in the damp, chilly air between us, giving him a moment to absorb where I'm going with this, but it doesn't seem to register.

"In that scene, *Le Chiffre* strips Bond naked, ties him to a chair with no seat on it, and then whips his junk with a large rope."

Ryan's head jerks up, and wide, frantic eyes meet mine. Things have finally fallen into place. He finally understands.

I grin at him and reach down to grab the old, weathered mooring rope beside the seatless chair he's strapped to. "Now you know why you're naked." I push to my feet and lean in. "I want to ensure you feel every damn bit of this in the place it will hurt the most."

"No! No! Please! I-I won't go near her again. I won't—"

Liar.

I swing the rope and whip the knotted end up and under the chair to slam against his dick and nuts. He cries out something unintelligible and lurches forward against the restraints keeping him upright.

"If you can't stop thinking with your dick, then we need to take it out of play."

If I can't take him out of play, I can at least punish him in a way he'll feel forever.

Very real, very permanent damage is likely—and would be most welcome. But it still isn't enough to ensure he won't continue to stalk Robyn and make her live in fear. And that's not something I'm willing to let happen to any innocent woman.

I take another swing, this time adding an exaggerated flick of my wrist at the end to ensure it gets up high and connects with one hundred percent of the force I intend it to.

Bloody vomit spews from his mouth, out across the floor and over my boots. I glance down at them and groan.

Dammit. These are so comfortable and broken in.

"Now I have to replace my boots, Ryan." I shake my head. "That doesn't make me very happy."

He chokes and gags again, heaving out breaths that are becoming more and more ragged. "I-I can-can't breathe..."

"I imagine not."

I know what it feels like to be gasping for breath. Not being able to fill your lungs. Your body struggling for oxygen, for what it needs to keep functioning. I've been there one too many times, and it's much more pleasant being on this side. But another blow like that might make him lose consciousness, and I need him alert to hear my words and understand them.

Gripping his hair again, I tug his head up. "Now is the time to listen and really pay attention, Ryan, since you didn't when we had our first chat..."

A strangled groan is the only response I get, but his eyes are open and somewhat focused. If I wait any longer, my message may be lost in his fogged brain.

"You will be leaving Baltimore." I twist my fingers in his hair tightly. "I will personally escort you out of town, and you will keep driving until you hit the Pacific. Then, you can drive straight into the water for all I care, but what you will *not* do is ever come back to Baltimore or the East Coast at all. Ever. It's off fucking limits to you. Do you understand me?"

He opens his mouth to speak, but only a struggled rush of air comes out.

"What did you say?"

I lean slightly toward him, tilting my head to the side to try to hear what he's saying. He swallows thickly, the sound wet with his own blood and saliva.

"I-I ca-can't leave. My job. My parents—"

"Are none of my fucking concern. What *is* my concern is the safety of Robyn Hall, and I'll be watching you, ensuring you keep to your side of the fucking country. And if there are any other *problems* like what happened here and other women being harassed, my face will be the one you wake up to just before you take your last breath. Are we clear?"

He coughs and sputters, the rattling sound in his chest more pronounced than before. "O-okay."

A smile pulls at my lips, and I release his hair, letting his head drop and his body sag forward against the ropes keeping him bound to the chair. "Then we're done here."

I walk away from him and out to the edge of the water, inhaling the fresh air while I pull my phone from my pocket and turn it on to call Reaper with an update on our client's problem. Ryan may look bad, but none of his injuries will prevent him from packing up and leaving town tonight. I made sure of that.

My phone glows to life, and the little red voicemail icon sits in the center of the screen.

What the hell?

No one has this number except Reaper, Mouth, and a handful of other guys from the unit. None of them would leave a message, and the number it came from isn't familiar.

I press the button to make it play and put the phone to my ear, staring at the glistening lights across the river.

A strangled sob floats through the line, driving straight to my heart. The agonized sound I've heard before from the same lips. Ones I used to kiss. "Kalen, I'm in trouble. I don't know what to do. I need you—"

The voicemail cuts out, and I tug the phone from my ear and call the number back.

"Hi, you've reached Avery Mills. I'm not available to

take your call right now, but leave a message, and I'll get back to you as soon as I can.

Beep.

That sharp sound pierces my ear, and I end the call as I try to suck in a breath against the vise suddenly tightening around my chest.

My always-steady hand shakes as I call Reaper and wait for him to answer.

He picks up on the second ring. "You done?"

"I need you to come meet me here to take care of the package. Avery's in trouble. I have to find her."

2

_____

CHAOS

The door to the condo stands slightly ajar, but no light trickles out from inside. This time of night, the area's quiet, still.

It should be comforting.

If any of the busybodies in the neighborhood watch heard or saw anything suspicious, they would have contacted the police, who would be here by now. Given the number of stickers and signs in windows around here, there are plenty of people watching, yet the night remains silent. Everyone completely oblivious to whatever went down at Avery's place.

Anyone else might have missed the door being open that fraction of an inch, might have walked by on the street and glanced up at it and not have noticed or given it a second thought. But I don't miss things like that.

When I do, people die.

Shaking off that thought, gun in hand, I nudge open the door and make my way inside. Her familiar scent hits me instantly—light, flowery, sweet. Perfect.

Just like her.

Overturned furniture...

Drawers dumped out...

Avery's belongings scattered around the living room...

And the kitchen...

I slowly make my way down the short hallway, listening for any signs that whoever did this might still be here, but the dead silence makes my blood run cold.

She isn't here, but someone else sure as hell was, and they may have left with what they wanted. The same thing I always wanted but never deserved and never should have had.

Fucking hell.

Her bedroom smells even *more* like her, and as I clear it, I inhale deeply, relishing what might be my last chance to experience it again.

I never thought I would after that night.

And if she hadn't called, I never would have.

The apartment is a wreck, but there isn't any trace of her or whoever might have done this.

Son of a bitch.

It's only been an hour since she left the message, so she's still close—assuming she called from here.

I hustle back to the front of her condo, close the

front door, flip on the lights, and pull out my phone. Hers goes straight to voicemail again.

Shit.

The phone is likely dead or turned off; otherwise, she would have called me back. But her car wasn't parked out front. I need help finding her, and there's only one person I know who has the skills to do it.

I quickly dial Preacher, and he answers on the third ring.

"Chaos, long time no talk."

It has been a while, but I don't have time for idle chit-chat or catching up with old friends. What I need is his very specific skillset.

"I can't find Avery." The words burn in my chest, and I absently rub at it. "I think somebody grabbed her."

"What happened?" All the humor and good cheer his greeting held flee instantly. "Tell me everything."

"She called me and left a message saying she was in trouble. Then it cut out. I'm at her place, where she moved after the divorce. No sign of her, but it's trashed."

"Oh, hell. What do you need?"

"Can you track her phone or her car? I'm texting you her number."

The sound of his fingers flying across the keyboard hits me. "Give me five minutes."

It's five minutes too long.

Every second that ticks by makes things more

dangerous for her—a truth Preacher knows as well as I do.

I send him the number and lower myself onto the couch, squeezing the bridge of my nose. The continued clicking of keys offers me a brief glimmer of hope that he might find something, and it's the only thing preventing me from completely going off the rails.

"Nothing on the phone. It's probably turned off or dead—"

"Shit."

"—but I got into the DMV database and located her car, then got the GPS tracker number from the dealership where she bought it. Wait a second..."

I hold my breath as more typing ticks in my head like a damn clock counting down.

"Got it. Traveling West on US 66 near Wellington."

I jerk my head up. "Are you sure?"

"Yeah. Why, do you know where she is?"

There's only one reason she'd be up there. Only one place she could go. And it makes complete sense. If she were in trouble, if she knew she couldn't come home, or if she came home to this, she would have taken off and headed somewhere she felt safe. Some-where she believed no one could find her—except maybe me.

"I know where she's going."

"Do you need assistance? I'm sure Cutter can get out there if you need him."

As much as I love the thought of having Cutter

Jackson at my side again, there isn't any time to wait for him to get here from Chicago, and Reaper and Mouth are tied up cleaning up Ryan and getting him out of town for our client. I'm on my own tonight.

"No. At least, not right now. I don't know what's going on yet. But as soon as I find out anything, I'll let you and Cutter know."

"If you need anything, just call." The sincerity in the computer genius' voice helps ease the tiniest bit of tension in my body. "And hey, Chaos?"

"What?"

"I hope your girl is okay."

I end the call.

My girl.

Avery hasn't been my girl in a long fucking time. And with good reason. The last words we spoke to each other were in anger. Awful, terrible, hate-filled words neither one of us can take back, said while lawyers sat at our sides and we signed the divorce papers.

Yet...she called *me.*

She didn't call 9-1-1. She didn't call the people you're supposed to call. She called the number I gave her all those years ago when we were still together and told her to use if she ever needed something, if she were ever in trouble.

I never thought she would. But she reached out.

Things must be really fucking bad for her to come to me.

I push to my feet and give the living room one last

scan. My eyes land on a framed photograph of her on a beach smiling bright, her auburn hair floating in the wind around her.

Damn. She looks good.

Even though I shouldn't, I walk over and pull it from the shelf. Examining it, for a moment, a twinge of jealousy heats my blood.

Who took this picture?

A boyfriend?

I swallow down that thought and quickly return the frame.

It doesn't matter. She needs *my* help, or she wouldn't have called.

I switch off the light, step out, and close the door behind me. I'll have to tell the guys to come back and get this cleaned up before anyone else discovers it and alerts the cops.

The last thing I need is them meddling in whatever this is and fucking up my chances of getting her back safely.

Scanning the street, I hustle down the stairs and back to my bike parked at the rear of the building. Straddling it, I pull on my helmet and take one final look at the place she settled when we split.

Not exactly the way I had hoped to see it.

But it wasn't like she was inviting me over for friendly chitchat after what went down.

I fire up the bike, knock up the kickstand, and tear out of the parking lot.

She may think she's heading somewhere safe, that

no one else can ever find her, but if *I* know she'd be there, someone else can easily figure it out, too.

Jesus, Avery, what have you gotten yourself into?

A million possibilities flit through my head as the cool wind whips around me, each worse than the last.

Whatever it is, I'm going to get you out.

AVERY

THE FAMILIAR NEON sign glowing in the distance makes me release the breath it feels like I've been holding for the last few hours while driving.

I made it.

Someone here will have a charger. I can get my phone working again and call Kalen to tell him where I am.

He'll just abandon you again, leave you twisting in the wind.

That tiny voice has been harping at me since I left the message for him, eating away slowly at the certainty I had that he would come to help me fix this horrible mess I've gotten myself into.

Kalen isn't the man I fell in love with. He hasn't been for a long time. All I really know is he has a history of letting me down, of failing me, of failing *us* so badly that it ended things.

I blink away another round of impending tears as I approach the gravel driveway for the diner. My stomach rumbles violently, a reminder I haven't eaten all day. The lack of calories mixed with the adrenaline coursing through my veins is finally starting to catch up with me. I can't ignore the lightheadedness I've been fighting for the last few miles.

As uneven and treacherous as the rest of the trip is from here, I definitely can't drive like this, but Bernice's chicken soup and homemade biscuits might just give me a tiny piece of comfort I need so badly after everything that's happened.

I put on my turn signal, even though the road is quiet and desolate behind me, and turn in to the almost-always empty parking lot.

This place is never exactly bustling. I can't recall it ever having more than five or six cars in the lot at any given time, except for maybe Christmas Eve. For some strange reason, that's when all the loonies from up the mountain come down for a drink.

Do they still do that?

It's been years since I've been up here, but everything still looks the same. The same chipping paint on the door boasts "hot coffee and pie — best in three counties," and despite everything that's happening, I find myself smiling because it really is.

Bernice's cooking can bring a smile to anyone. I'm proof of that. I should be a sobbing, shaking mess— and I *am*—but just imagining that familiar taste is enough to give me hope that this will somehow all work out.

I park facing the highway and inhale another deep

breath to try to keep myself in control. If I walk in there looking like this, Bernice will know something's wrong, and she cares enough to call the cops if she thinks I'm in any danger.

She would think she's helping, believe she's doing the right thing, but getting the authorities involved will only complicate things more.

It's why I need Kalen.

You don't need Kalen. You need Chaos.

My hands tighten around the wheel. That's a realization I don't want to consider right now. Not when Chaos is what changed him and destroyed us.

I look back at the broken window behind me and then at the diner, ensuring it isn't in view. If she happens to look out, she won't see the damage to my car, so I'm in the clear.

At least with that...

Keeping myself from blurting out the reality of this mess once I see her will be harder than this drive was. Bernice has a way of drawing things out of you, things you never thought you'd reveal.

Not today, Bernice.

All I need is soup. Not a heart-to-heart.

I climb from the car, phone in hand, and beeline for the glass door. Pulling it open, bells jingle overhead and a familiar head of white hair lifts from behind the counter to examine the newest arrival.

"Well, Avery Marie Mills, is that you?" Bernice grins at me and races around the counter even though I haven't answered.

I swallow back the sob that threatens to climb up my throat and instead force a smile. "Hi, Bernice. It's good to see you."

"Oh, honey." She pulls me into her arms, gifting me a warm hug I haven't felt in years. Pulling back, she examines me, pressing her palms against my cheeks. "Honey, you look upset. Is something wrong?"

"No, no, I'm okay."

If I believe it, so will she.

She narrows her shrewd russet gaze on me. "What are you doing up here now?" Her eyes dart to the clock. "And this late! It's been what...five years since you've stopped by and you decided to at midnight?"

"About that, yeah." I offer a shrug I hope comes across as nonchalant. "I just needed to spend some time up here."

"Well, I'm glad you stopped." She drops her hands to my shoulders and gives them a squeeze. "I just made a fresh batch of your favorite soup. And I have an apple pie about ready to come out of the oven."

True warmth spreads through me for the first time tonight, flooding me with good memories of times when things felt so certain and safe. "That sounds great." I hold up my phone. "Do you happen to have a charger that would work on this phone?"

She examines it and chews her lip. "You know, I'm not quite sure. All this technology stuff is way beyond me." She flits a hand. "But Russell is working in the kitchen, and he knows a hell of a lot more about this than I do. Let me go check with him while I grab your stuff."

"Thank you. I'm going to go use the bathroom."

An icy-cold splash of water on my face will do me good. Even though my hands have finally stopped shaking, knowing Bernice and her grandson are here with me, I still feel on edge, like a single word from her will break me open and I'll spill all my secrets.

That can't happen.

She winks at me. "Well, you know where it is."

"I sure do."

Almost fifteen years of spending summers up here at Grandpa's cabin made it like a second home, and coming to the diner for some soup and pie a few times a week while I was up here was an unbreakable tradition.

Part of me always suspected something was going on between Grandpa and Bernice all those years ago. The old widower and the old widow spent an awful lot of time together and shared a look every once in a while that I was too young to understand then, but now, looking back on it, I'm glad Gramps had someone like Bernice in his life.

It's hard going it alone, not having anyone to rely on or confide in.

Please don't fail me, Kalen.

I cast a quick glance out the big front window toward the road that brought me up the mountain. A pair of headlights approach, traveling the same direction I just was, and I hold my breath. The vehicle moves closer and closer, and anxiety coils coldly around my spine. Finally, the car hits the driveway for the diner, but it drives past it without slowing and disappears up the two-lane county highway farther up the mountain.

Oh, thank God.

My relieved sigh rushes from my lips, and I make my way to the short back hall that leads to the bathrooms and the rear exit. I push into the bathroom, do my business, and step out to wash my hands.

No wonder Bernice said I looked upset. Red rims my eyes despite my best efforts to stop the tears, and blotchy skin and wind-tangled hair from the broken car window make me look like something that just crawled out of the swamp.

Hell...

I wash my hands and splash cold water onto my face, then run my wet fingers through my hair, trying to tame the beast it has become. It doesn't do much good, but I look more human than I did a few minutes ago. Not even close to perfect, but it's the best I can do.

Bernice's soup and pie will help, too. The kind of cooking that can make any rainy day—or murderous one—better.

I step out of the bathroom to return to the main portion of the diner, and a hand wraps around my waist tightly from behind while another flattens over my mouth, stifling my attempt to scream.

3

AVERY

I try to scream again, but the large hand over my mouth muffles any attempt to cry for help to Bernice or Russell. My attacker drags me backward, and despite my best attempts to grip the door frame and keep him from doing it, he yanks me out the rear exit of the diner easily, as if I weigh nothing and my thrashing doesn't faze him.

But he's not going to take me easily.

Never.

After all that's happened in the last few hours to get me here, I refuse to let this asshole win.

I reach back toward his head and try to find his eyes with my thumbs to gouge them as I kick his shin with my left foot with all the strength I have. He squeezes his eyes shut against my assault, and his hold doesn't loosen even a bit with the strike to his leg, but our movement stops just outside the door.

Warm breath floats across the back of my neck and right ear, making me shudder and gag against the hand.

"I taught you well. That would have worked on anyone else." Kalen's deep, husky voice rolls over me like a soothing balm, bringing with it years of memories—of promises made and broken, of a love I thought was going to last forever but crumbled so easily under the weight of the world he carried on his shoulders as Chaos.

The hand around my mouth slides off, and he squeezes me around the waist once and releases me. I whirl around to face him and meet his ice-cold blue stare.

So many years have passed since I last saw his face, and then, it was through a haze of tears. But the ones burning my eyes now aren't of despair like they were that night. They aren't from fear of him even though he looks harder, like life has beaten him up over and over again and left him barely hanging by a thread. They're because he's really *here*. It's *him*. It's Kalen.

And once—what feels like not that long ago, standing here with him so close—he was my entire world.

"Oh, my God! Kalen!" I launch myself at him, throwing my arms around his neck as his strong ones wrap around me and hold me tightly. A sob slips from my lips, and I fight another one as a million words try to race out at once. "How did you find me? My phone is dead and—"

"*Shh.*" He pulls me against the side of the diner and takes my face between his palms abruptly. "Quiet."

It's an order—clipped and direct.

He scans the area where we hide at the rear of the restaurant, assessing every noise, every movement of an animal in the woods behind us, searching for threats.

The hair on the back of my neck stands on end, and I whip my head around, trying to see what he does. "W-what's wrong?"

He leans to the side and glances around the corner of the building toward the front parking lot where I left my car. "Just making sure we don't have any unexpected company." He turns to me and sighs. "I found you way too easily. After I couldn't call you back, I had a friend of mine try to track your phone and your car's GPS."

"You can do that?"

"Not legally, but I would have figured out you were here, anyway." His hard glare softens slightly. "Your grandfather's cabin was always a haven for you. It's the first place I would have looked...which means whoever you're running from will look there, too. We're not safe here—"

What?

"But no one else knows about it. How can anybody know I'm here?"

He raises a dark eyebrow, a move he always used

when he was biting back saying something he knew would start a fight. "You never told *anyone* about your grandfather's place?"

"What? No, of course not." A memory flickers in my head. Two years ago...well before I understood how much danger I was in working there. "Oh, shit."

Kalen takes a step toward me, concern furrowing his brow. "What?"

"I *did*. A couple of the guys in the office were talking about going deep-sea fishing in Mexico, and I commented that I loved to fish. They were really surprised and asked where I had fished—"

"And you told him up here with your grandfather at his cabin."

I nod and groan. "Yeah. Oh, my God. What if they're—"

Headlights sweep across the side of the building closest to us, and Kalen grabs me and shoves me behind him as he pulls a weapon from a holster at his hip.

I try to see over his shoulder, but his wide body blocks me almost completely. "What is it?"

He peeks around the corner, steady as a rock, observing. Assessing. Analyzing the way he was trained to. "A dark sedan just pulled into the parking lot."

Acid churns in my empty stomach and climbs up my throat. "Maybe they're just coming in for some pie."

Maybe it's just wishful thinking on my part, but if it's the people I'm running from, then I'm not the only one in danger. Bernice and Russell are sitting ducks in the diner, and I have first-hand knowledge that these guys are not afraid to get their hands dirty and bloody to get what they want. They wouldn't think twice about torturing innocent people to locate me.

Kalen makes a disgusted noise in his throat. "They're not here for *pie*, Avery. They're approaching your car."

"Shit. What do we do?"

He glances at me. "*You're* not gonna do *anything*. *You're* gonna stay *right* there. Don't move. Don't say a word. No matter what you hear."

Oh, God. No matter what I hear?

I grip his forearm tightly and tug until he peeks back at me again. "What are you going to do?"

His eyes darken from blue to almost black, his face hardening like granite. The shift from Kalen to Chaos is almost instant, and it makes me release his arm and retreat a tiny half-step.

"I'm going to do whatever the fuck I need to do to eliminate the threat."

He doesn't need to expand on that any further, and if I open my mouth with any sort of objection, it will only make things worse between us. Challenging him when he's in "Chaos mode" and intent on destruction always did.

I don't know what I expected when I called him for help, but seeing him like this—seeing *Chaos*, the part of the man that broke up everything we once shared— chills me to the core.

Wrapping my arms around myself, I shiver and fight another sob. "You're going to kill them."

It isn't a question because I know the answer. He won't give them a chance to survive, to return to their boss, to come after me again. He will *end* the threat. It's what he *does*.

He presses his lips into a hard line. "I don't know what you've gotten yourself into, Avery, but do you want my fucking help or not?"

I nod quickly.

That's Chaos.

There's the man I need in this moment.

Not the warm arms to embrace me but the cold hands that can kill easily.

"Stay here and don't fucking move. Do you hear me?"

CHAOS

AVERY NODS AT ME, her green eyes wide with fear that makes her entire body shake like the ground is quaking beneath her feet. Her bottom lip quivers, and she pulls it between her teeth, likely to try to keep herself from crying.

It's what she always did when she didn't want to appear weak or affected by something, but she can't hide it now. Not from me. I know her too well.

Whatever's going on is bad. Bad enough that she's

running for her life. This isn't just some misunderstanding or some argument with a friend. She's terrified, and after what I saw at her condo, rightfully so.

Someone is after something she has, and it appears they'll stop at nothing to get it.

What the hell *have you gotten yourself into, Avery?*

Whatever it is, these fuckers seem pretty damn determined, and I need to get a better look. I creep along the side of the building to where a large glass window looks into the diner, and I can see through the front window straight into the parking lot.

The black sedan stops behind Avery's car, and the two men inside lean toward it to examine it. They exchange a few words and look toward the building.

Shit.

If they go in there, looking for her, innocent people are going to get pulled into this mess.

Knowing how deeply Avery cares about Bernice, if anything happens to her, Avery will never forgive herself, never recover, even if I manage to save her from whoever is after her.

I duck down and race below the window to the corner of the diner as they pull in and park next to Avery's car. Two men, clearly packing some serious heat, given the bumps under their shirts at their sides, scan their surroundings. One reaches in through a broken window of the car while the other watches the diner.

They're still looking for something, but it appears he doesn't find it. He rises from the window, and the two start to move across the parking lot toward the restaurant.

I fire off four quick rounds—two into each—before they even have time to react, the sound of the shots reverberating off the mountains around us. They hit the pavement almost simultaneously, and an eerie silence falls over the area. I hustle to where Avery stands near the back door, grab her hand, and pull her in the direction of the other side of the building.

"We need to move."

She glances at the building as I drag her toward the woods behind it. "What about Bernice? We can't just leave her. They'll—"

I tighten my grip on her hand to keep her from trying to slip out of my hold and go back. "They're not going to hurt Bernice."

"What?" Her voice cracks on the word, and she shakes her head. "How can you know that?"

My feet pound on the uneven ground, and she stumbles along behind me—going back through the woods the same way I came in. "Because they're *dead*, Avery."

"Dead?" She looks back toward the diner, now partially concealed by the bushes and trees. "Are you sure?"

I pause for a second and turn toward her, our bodies mere centimeters from each other. "I'm fucking *sure*, Avery, and now, we gotta go."

"Where?"

"Somewhere safe. Somewhere they won't trace

back to you so you can tell me what the fuck is going on and explain what you've gotten yourself into."

It doesn't make any sense. Avery has always toed the line, always followed the rules, never even sped on the damn highway, which is how I was able to catch up to her. She's never been a rule breaker and never stepped on anyone else's toes or nosed into anyone else's business. Yet, here we are...

No matter how hard I try, I just can't wrap my head around what she could have done to have someone after her like this. But once we get to my place, she's going to tell me *everything.*

I lead her over to my bike, hidden behind a patch of thorny bushes where I left it so no one would hear or see me when I came up to the diner.

Her eyes widen slightly. "What about my car?"

I grip her wrist and draw her up against me. The low growl in my chest comes out before I can even stop it. "That's how I so easily tracked you. If they have the right resources at their disposal, they'll be able to use the GPS the same way I did. Where's your phone?"

She reaches into her pocket with a shaky hand and holds it up.

"Give it to me."

"But it's dead."

I glare at her until she hands it over, then I release her wrist and chuck it against the ground and stomp my boot against it with a satisfying crunch.

"No!" Avery lunges toward the shattered phone, dropping to her knees. "We need that."

"What do you mean?"

Bordering on frantic now, she tries to gather the pieces. "There's information on the phone. Something we need."

Fuck.

The SIM card wasn't really a problem since the phone was dead, but I couldn't have her bring it back and plug it in to charge it up.

I squat and help her scoop up the pieces of the phone until I find the memory card. Meeting her gaze, I hold up the tiny piece of plastic. "Should all be on here."

She releases a heavy, relieved sigh and watches me shove it into my pocket. I grab the remains of the phone from her hand and toss them onto the ground, except for the SIM card. That, I place on a rock and stomp on it until it breaks.

"Now, we gotta go."

Whatever is going on, the longer we stay here, the greater chance the police will arrive and tie us to the two bodies lying on the pavement in front of the diner before we're far enough away to escape them. As it stands, once they run her plates, they'll be looking for Avery. But we can deal with that later. Right now, the only thing that matters is getting us somewhere safe so she can tell me everything.

I hold out my hand, and she accepts it, letting me pull her up from the ground. Even out here, surrounded by nature, her scent wraps around me and invades my lungs. I tried to ignore it earlier, tried to push it away and concentrate on my mission, but something tells me that's going to be nearly impossible with Avery at the center of it.

Her eyes lock with mine for a moment, and I force myself to look away and climb onto the bike. "Get on."

She throws her leg over behind me, just like she has hundreds of times, and I hand her my helmet without looking back. Having Avery with me on my motorcycle again is a dream and a living nightmare.

Thin arms wrap around my waist, and she lays her head against my shoulder blade. Her entire body shakes violently, and I start the ignition. It rumbles beneath us, and almost instantly, she relaxes into me.

Fuck.

I need to get her somewhere safe.

Somewhere away from *me*.

4

CHAOS

Trying to concentrate on the rumble of the road beneath us or the harsh wind whipping at me as we fly down the road on our way back to the city doesn't help distract me from every shift Avery makes behind me. The way she clings to me so tightly, like I'm the most important thing in the world. The same way she always used to before I ruined everything.

I never thought I'd see her again, let alone have her wrapped around me on the open road for hours like she used to be, as if no time has passed, like all the turmoil and hurt simply blew away in the wind floating around us. It's dangerous to relish it, to wish it could stay like this forever, but now that I have finally reached my place, I almost regret the ride wasn't longer, even though I know the safest thing to do is get inside and figure out what the fuck is going on.

Any delay just gives more time to whoever is after her to figure out a way to track her down. Plus, Bernice undoubtedly called the police when she heard the gunshots and discovered two bodies in her parking lot with Avery missing.

Thank fuck that old place doesn't have surveillance cameras.

Eventually, we'll have to come up with a story explaining what happened, but that isn't an immediate concern. Keeping Avery safe is.

I park my bike, knock down the kickstand, and kill the engine. Avery's death grip on me relaxes before she shifts on the seat. An awkward moment stretches out between us—neither of us saying anything or moving. Finally, I glance over my shoulder at her, and she pulls off the helmet, releasing her dark, disheveled hair.

My fingers itch to run through it, to smooth it away from her face, tuck it behind her ear, and I flex them at my sides to try to dispel the feeling, letting my gaze linger on the tiny cuts along the side of her face left from the blown-out window of her car.

Seeing the injury on her makes me want to go back and kill those fuckers again. Once I find out who is responsible, I'll be able to unleash all this anger some-where because I don't want to direct it at Avery.

She offers me a tiny half smile. "It's been a long time since I've ridden on one of these."

That shouldn't make relief flood through my system, but it does.

She hasn't been on any other asshole's ride in the time since we split.

Thank fuck.

I couldn't handle knowing she had been. It's hard enough trying not to think about all the other things she's likely been up to since we ended things.

She shifts to slide off the seat, and I offer her my hand to help her. A ride like that after so many years off a bike is bound to have made her sore. She places her small, soft hand in mine, and a tiny little zing shoots up my arm and goes straight to my cock.

Fucking hell.

Avery always did that to me, and it appears our time apart hasn't changed anything. It takes her a moment to find her footing, but as soon as she's steady, I jerk my hand from hers and motion toward the steps on the side of the building leading up to my second-floor apartment.

"Let's go."

I climb off while I scan the street behind us, watching for anything suspicious or out of the ordinary, but the entire area is quiet. It tends to be this early in the morning, just before sunrise. None of the businesses surrounding my building will open until at least eight, and there isn't anything else to bring anyone down here this time of day.

Exactly why I chose this place.

Avery pauses at the bottom of the steps, looking to

her left at the row of garage doors and the sign above them. "What is this place?

"A car and motorcycle repair shop. I live above it. Go!"

She complies without offering another comment, and I follow her up the stairs, her tight ass encased in perfectly form-fitting jeans taunting me right in front of my face with each step. I have to bite back the desire to reach up and smack it like I used to every time we were in this position before.

This isn't then, and she isn't yours anymore.

That was my choice. My actions drove her away, and I have to live with the consequences, even if it was necessary. That means ignoring the urge to touch her, to feel her against me, to take what used to be mine.

She pauses at the top of the stairs on the tiny landing outside the single door that leads to my apartment, and I pull out my keys and unlock the deadbolt, pushing it open for her to enter ahead of me.

I'm not letting Avery out of my damn sight until all this is resolved.

Avery slowly steps inside, and I usher her in farther with a hand on her lower back and flip the light switch. The single bulb hanging from the sad, ancient fixture in the center of the room flickers to life, and she pauses just inside the living room while I lock the door.

She scans the space quickly, then turns back to me with her eyebrow raised. "How long have you lived here?"

I offer a shrug. "Couple of years."

"Where's all your stuff?"

The single recliner sits in one corner, the television hanging opposite. Otherwise, the room is empty.

Just the way I like it.

I shrug again. "I have everything I need."

It's a lie I constantly tell myself, which is why I don't look at Avery when I say the words, just push past her into the small kitchen. Having her here, letting her see me live like this, so different from the warm, welcoming home we once shared, makes my shoulders tighten.

"Aren't you worried somebody might find us here and come looking for me?"

I freeze in front of the fridge and turn slowly to face her. "In order for them to do that, they would have to know who I was and how we were connected. And I bet you never told anybody you were ever married."

Her face falls slightly, and she gulps, averting her gaze to her feet for a second and shifting nervously on her feet. "I didn't."

"Exactly." I turn and grab a beer from the fridge, knock off the cap, and bring it to my lips. "So, no one knows who I am."

It's no surprise she didn't say anything about me to anyone. It isn't an experience she wants to relive, even if just through memories.

She slowly lifts her head. "I didn't tell anyone about you because it was too painful for me."

Her words hit me the same way the bullets did those two fuckers in the parking lot back at the diner, and I take a long pull from the bottle to give me a distraction from the ache in my chest. But the cool, hoppy liquid doesn't help wash away the hurt of the truth in what she said.

Like I need more reminders of how I destroyed every-thing. How badly I destroyed her...

I stare at the bottle for a moment, down half the beer, then pull out my phone and dial Reaper.

It only rings once before he picks up. "Hey, man. Status?"

"I'm fine. I have her, and she's okay." I glance over at Avery, where she shifts back and forth on her feet in the middle of my barren living room. "We're at my place. I need you guys to come over to figure out a plan for taking care of her situation."

"We handled our other problem. Got him out of town."

That douchebag, stalker asshole.

It would have been great to be there to watch him leave the city and drive away in agony after the way I worked him over, but given how shaken Avery is, it was the right decision to ditch the dumbass and go get her.

"Good."

"We'll be over there soon."

I end the call, slide my phone into my pocket, and take another swig of my beer.

Avery watches me tentatively, pulling her bottom lip between her teeth and twisting her hands in front of her. "Who did you call?"

I set down the bottle and lay my hands flat on the

counter, leaning against it, happy it puts some much-needed distance between us—a barrier on top of the one I've already erected through my actions in the past. "Reaper and Mouth."

She winces, and her lips twist down. "I'm really not comfortable having them involved with this."

Her reaction churns my gut for multiple reasons. There was a time when she was their friend, when she trusted them with her life the way she trusted me. But now they're the enemy as much as I've become. I was a last-resort call, and that truth makes me slam my palm against the cheap formica.

It causes her to jump, and I instantly regret having scared her when she's already so terrified, but I need her to focus and understand the position she's in.

"You called *me* for help, Avery. You don't get to decide how I do it. Now, tell me what the *hell* is going on."

AVERY

HIS ANGER IS WARRANTED. I've dragged him into a massive clusterfuck, and now I've insulted his friends. I never should have said anything, no matter how uneasy seeing them will make me.

They became everything to him when I became nothing. All he wanted was to be with them, to be Chaos as they saw him. They're the last people I want to see; still, I should keep my mouth shut about it rather than make an already-uncomfortable situation even more so by basically insulting them.

I'd love to crawl into a hole and hide now—from the reality of what's happening and from the look Kalen is giving me—but I don't have any choice but to tell him everything, to tell him what I saw.

It's the only chance I have of maybe getting out of this alive.

My hands shake as I wander over to the only piece of furniture in the room—the battered, beat-up old recliner he always loved so much. Just like us, the years have done more damage to it—the leather torn in spots and rubbed almost bare in others. Scars that match the ones we bear.

Without looking at Kalen, I slowly lower myself into it. "So...after we split, I sold the house."

"I know." His voice comes harsh and abrupt, like thinking about the home we once shared is just as painful for him as it is for me. "I wanted you to keep it."

"Well, I used the money from the sale to go back to school and get a degree in accounting. I needed some way to support myself, a job, and I wasn't qualified to do anything since I never worked before—"

"You didn't have to work. Every damn month, I sent my check to your bank account so you would always be taken care of and you wouldn't have to work."

I glance over at him, the anger burning in his gaze making me shift on the chair. "I didn't want your money. After we split, I didn't want anything to do with you. I wanted to support myself on my own. I haven't touched a *dime* of what you've sent me over the last four years. It's all still sitting in that account. You can have it."

Kalen's jaw tightens, and he fists his hands on the top of the narrow counter separating us. "What the hell, Avery?"

"I needed to do something on my own. *Be* on my own. So..."—I try to draw us away from this conversation because it's only going to get more painful if we go down that road further—"I got my degree in accounting, and I got a job at a food service company. You know, they provide products to restaurants and schools and things like that."

He nods, though it doesn't appear any of his anger or annoyance has faded.

"I was helping with the accounting. The owner also has some restaurants. It was busy. Another woman, her name was Amelia, she had been working for him for a while, and I was basically brought on to assist her."

Her kind, warm, bourbon eyes flash in my head, and I bite back a sob that threatens to slip from my lips. "Then, a month or two ago, she started acting strange."

"Strange how?"

I glance over at Kalen to find him slightly more relaxed, taking a sip of his beer. "Just...off?" I shrug. "She wasn't as talkative as usual, and she took back a lot of tasks she had previously asked me to take care of, almost like she didn't trust me to do it anymore. Now, I know what it really was…"

"What happened, Avery?"

"Yesterday morning, I went into the office like usual, and she wasn't there. That was weird because she was an early riser and always one of the first ones in. The owner, Ricardo Perez, told me she had decided to retire early and move back to the small town in Mexico where her family still lived."

"Okay…"

"But something just felt off about that. She had been telling me about how she needed to work for a few more years to really be comfortable retiring. She cared for her elderly parents and helped some other family members financially, so she really wanted a nice nest egg built up and wasn't there yet."

He considers my explanation for a moment. "So, you didn't buy what he was telling you?"

"No, but I didn't want to challenge my boss and maybe get fired, and I didn't really have any reason to suspect anything was wrong other than the *off* feeling. Until…" I sigh and brush my hair back from my face with shaking hands. "Until I moved into her bigger office later in the day, at Ricardo's suggestion, and I found a thumb drive taped to the underside of the desk."

Kalen freezes, the bottle in his hand. "What was on it?"

"At first, I was confused. I put it into the computer and

didn't know what I was looking at. It took me a while to realize she had prepared it, that it was comparisons of numbers. Inventory, sales, cash coming in from the restaurants and the customers who made purchases from the supply side of the business as well as expenses paid out." I lock eyes with Kalen. "None of it matched up."

"What do you mean?"

"There was a whole lot of cash coming from somewhere. It shouldn't have been there. There were customer names I didn't recognize. At first, I thought I was just missing something, not understanding what I was looking at. I took it home last night to examine it more carefully because I didn't want to jump to any conclusions if there was a reasonable explanation and didn't want my boss mad at me for messing up the books if there was an issue."

"But there wasn't a reasonable explanation?"

I shake my head. "Not one I could find. I Googled the names of the companies supposedly making purchases from us, but they either didn't exist or had very basic information on their websites that made it look like they weren't real. So, I went back to the office late last night. Ricardo had always been weird about that—us working late. He said he didn't expect us to and that he wanted us to have real lives. I never thought anything of it. I never really questioned why he wouldn't want anyone there after hours."

Idiot.

Naïve fool.

What boss discourages *employees from working a little harder and staying to finish things?*

Only one who is hiding something.

Kalen's jaw tenses as he listens. He's thinking the same damn thing I should have immediately. One thing he always taught me was to be aware of my surroundings, to keep my eyes and ears open for anything off. He always said intuition was our strongest weapon.

And I ignored mine.

"Ricardo's car was parked outside the building that housed our offices, but he wasn't in there. There were some more vehicles by the connected warehouse, which I found odd since I didn't realize anyone ever worked late besides him. I walked over to the warehouse to look for him and..."

"And what?"

"I—" My words catch in my throat as the memories of what I saw flash in vivid red before my eyes. "He-he was there with some of the delivery men, but they weren't working on packing the trucks with items for deliveries."

"What were they doing?"

A single tear drops down my cheek. "It just seemed suspicious, odd there would be workers there late at night. Something was off. I initially didn't see Ricardo from where I stood just inside the dock door, so I thought maybe they were stealing from the company." I let out a shaky breath. "But the truth was so much worse."

"Just tell me, Avery."

"They pulled Amelia's body from one of the freezers and loaded it into the back of a truck." I choke back a sob and squeeze my eyes closed. "There was so much blood all over her. He-he killed her because she had discovered whatever the hell he was doing."

I try to swallow another sob and force the words out, but all that comes is a wail that sounds almost inhuman from somewhere deep in my chest.

Strong, warm arms wrap around me and hold me steady. The familiarity of his embrace, the feeling of absolute safety, makes me forget all the reasons this is the wrong place to be, that he's the wrong person to be with. Instead, I drape my arms around his neck and weep against his shoulder, letting go of everything I have left in me, everything I've tried so hard to ignore and keep inside while I fight for my life.

Kalen pulls back my head, and his hard eyes meet mine. "What's on the phone that's so important?"

I take a deep inhale. "When I realized they were doing something sketchy, I pulled out my phone, and I recorded it."

His dark eyebrows rise slowly. "You got video of them moving the body?"

"Yeah."

"What about the zip drive with the numbers? Where is it now?"

"It's still at the office. I left it on my desk."

Kalen's lips twist into a frown. "Shit. That's not why they're after you, though."

"No. I don't know how they could know I had the drive or that it even existed. They must have figured out I was watching them, or someone saw me there recording before I ran and drove away. They're trying to kill me, Kalen. One of the men from the warehouse followed me and tried to ram my car, and now, those two at the diner..."

"Why didn't you call the police or go straight to the police station?"

"Because one of the men in the warehouse was wearing a police uniform, and a squad car was parked outside the dock doors. I saw it when I was leaving."

"Fuck."

I suck in a shaky breath, fighting another sob filling my chest.

Kalen rests his large hands on my thighs and squeezes. "I'm not going to let anything happen to you. I promise."

"How can you say that? These men...they're obviously dangerous. Wherever this money is coming from, it's something bad. I—"

He captures my face between his palms and forces me to meet his concerned gaze. "I know, but I'm very good at what I do. You have to trust me."

That's far easier said than done, given our history. He's broken so many promises, shattered me in so many ways. It's hard to believe anything he says anymore.

But I'll try.

What other choice do I have?

5

AVERY

People always talk about adrenaline crashes. How you ride the high until you finally collapse to a crushing low and an exhaustion that permeates deep in your bones.

I finally understand what they mean.

It hits me within half an hour of walking into Kalen's place and unloading the weight of what I saw. Between being curled up in the old recliner that was always so comfortable, the last of the adrenaline that's been keeping me going wearing off, and Kalen standing vigil over me, I finally let my eyes drift closed.

I let myself go and try to forget the vivid, horrific recent memory for just a few moments. It's quickly replaced with a good memory, one of the many Kalen and I had before everything changed, before *he* changed.

The beach...

The shining sun beating down on us, warming our exposed skin...

Him kissing his way across my flat belly to my lips and capturing my mouth in a way that says if we weren't in public, surrounded by hundreds of other beachgoers, he'd be taking me right now on the sand...

Instead, he pries his lips from mine and grins at me, his eyes covered by his sunglasses. "What are we gonna do for the rest of the day? Because I have some ideas."

I chuckle and push at his shoulder. "You're terrible."

"What?" One of his eyebrows rises over the reflective lenses. "What's so wrong with wanting to go back to the hotel and fuck my wife mindless?"

Shaking my head, I return his grin. "Nothing. Except that's all we've been doing in the last two days. And I actually want to *do* something on our honeymoon besides you fucking me mindless, if you don't mind."

"Oh, I *do* mind..." He captures my mouth again. His greedy tongue slips between my lips, and he shifts his body tighter against mine. The fact that we're on a beach in Mexico, surrounded by other tourists, doesn't seem to faze him. It seems nothing does or can...

A hard knock at the door jerks me awake, and a high-pitched scream fills the tiny apartment.

"Avery, it's fine. You're okay." Kalen lays a hand on my shoulder and squeezes gently. "It's just the guys."

Hell, that was me screaming.

I push my hair away from my face and try to take controlled breaths to keep my heart from beating straight out of my chest.

Kalen makes his way over to the door, checks the peephole, and pulls it open to let Reaper and Mouth walk in. Each of the men offers me a nod of acknowledgment and nothing more.

Seems the hard feelings have carried over all this time.

That shouldn't surprise me. They would back up Kalen on anything, no questions asked. That kind of loyalty is necessary in their line of work. I'm the villain in this situation because I'm the one who served him papers. It doesn't matter that he's the one who really ended things.

Kalen starts to shut the door, and an arm slips through it.

A dark-haired woman with striking green eyes shoves her way through the jamb, an exasperated twist to her mouth. "Hey, don't close the door on me, asshole."

He groans and takes a step back to let her come fully into the apartment while casting an annoyed look at Reaper and Mouth. "Really?"

Reaper shrugs. "You try keeping her from coming."

Kalen scowls at the woman who holds up a plastic bag and jiggles it in front of him.

"For your information, I come bearing basic essentials since I figured she doesn't have anything, and you would be woefully unprepared for having a woman here." She chuckles at her own joke and nudges him playfully on the shoulder as she passes by. "Am I right?"

Who the hell is this woman?

Her eyes land on me, and she offers a kind smile and approaches with her hand extended. "Hi, I'm Viktoria, Reaper's..." She looks at him with a raised dark eyebrow. "Girlfriend, I guess? I'm also a former NYPD detective, so it's not completely out of the question that I might be able to offer some assistance in this situation." She glares at Kalen, who just stomps back to the kitchen and opens another beer silently. "Despite what *some people* might think."

Reaper leans in and whispers something into Viktoria's ear.

She nods and hands me the bag. "Here. Toothbrush and clean underwear. I didn't know your sizes and didn't want to bring you stuff you couldn't wear, so anything else you need I can bring by later. Just make a list for me."

"Oh, okay. Thanks. That's really nice of you."

I hadn't even thought about the fact that I have absolutely nothing with me. Everything I own is in my apartment.

Will I ever be able to go back?

That thought brings another wave of anxiety that tightens my chest.

Viktoria reaches out and offers me a quick squeeze on the shoulder, then glances around. "Wow, Chaos, you really know how to decorate a place to make it warm and inviting."

He takes a long pull off his beer and sneers at her. "Fuck you, Vik."

She snorts a laugh. "I don't think Reaper would appreciate that very much."

Reaper waves a hand between them and leans back against the wall since there isn't anywhere to sit. "Will you two knock it off for a minute so we can talk about business?" He turns his attention to me. "This isn't exactly how I thought I'd see you again. Want to fill us in on whatever mess you got yourself into?"

These are the last guys I want to come to begging for help, but they're the ones who are probably in the best position to actually *do* something about it.

I take a deep breath. "Long story short, I'm an accountant and I work for a food company. You know one of the places that supplies product to local restaurants and has some of their own."

Everyone nods.

"The woman who headed the accounting department disappeared, and then I discovered a flash drive she had hidden with documentation that made it look like a whole ton of money was coming into the company that shouldn't be."

Reaper glances at Kalen with a raised brow. "Money laundering? Drug trafficking."

He shrugs. "Could be both."

"Okay, continue, Avery."

"So, I went to talk to my boss about it after hours, which he always discouraged, but I never really understood why. And when I got there, I saw some of his men acting suspiciously in the warehouse. Something felt off, so I started recording on my phone, and..." I suck in a deep breath. "And I saw them pull the body of my coworker out of one of the freezers."

"Holy hell." Viktoria pushes off where she was leaning on the wall. "I'm going to need one of those beers."

Kalen glowers at her but turns back to the fridge and grabs her a bottle. "Mouth, you want one?"

Mouth shakes his head and continues watching me stoically.

When no one says anything, I keep going. "I didn't know what to do. I ran, and I left the drive there."

Reaper winces. "Shit."

"But I have the recording from the warehouse on my phone. As I was basically fleeing the scene of a murder, one of the men from the warehouse tried to ram my car and almost killed me at a busy intersection. Then he shot at me."

Viktoria takes a sip of her beer and casts a worried look at the guys. "So, they know you saw them."

"We have security cameras outside, so they may have been able to look at the video after the fact and see that I was there, or they may have seen me actually in the warehouse."

Reaper gives me a grim look. "And that you were recording them."

"Maybe." I shrug, everything about last night becoming a blur the more tired I become. "I don't know what they know, just that they apparently want me dead."

Kalen nods. "She was smart enough not to go home."

I glance at him. "I knew if they were determined enough to follow me and try to ram me with a car, then shoot at me in public, they would just end up at my place eventually."

Viktoria offers me a sympathetic smile. "Why didn't you just go straight to the police station?"

"Because one of the men in the warehouse was in a police uniform, and a squad car was parked in front."

One of Viktoria's dark eyebrows wings up. "You think he was involved?"

"He had to be because he watched them drag Amelia's body out and didn't even react. I don't think I can trust the cops. I headed out to my grandfather's cabin. He left it to me when he died, and I didn't think anyone would know about it except maybe Kalen."

Kalen steps out from behind the small counter and leans against it. "But I intercepted her at a little diner a few miles from his place. And none too soon. I had only been there five minutes before her friends from the warehouse showed up, looking for her. They won't be a problem anymore. At least, those two won't. But we need a game plan. We need to figure out who the players are and how to stop them. Get them off her back."

Viktoria looks between us. "Don't any of you think they're going to come here looking for her? I mean, you're her ex-husband. Shouldn't that be one of the first places they check?"

The look Kalen gives me makes me wince.

I shake my head. "No one there knew I was ever married."

Kalen downs the rest of his beer in one long pull. "Even if they went to the trouble of tracking down our marriage certificate, they would never find this place because my name isn't attached to it. I pay cash, and the guy who owns the shop downstairs doesn't even know my real name. This is the safest place she can be right now."

At least when it comes to hiding from Ricardo and his men.

Reaper shifts his weight, still leaning back against the wall. "We need everything you know about the business—owner, employees, customers. We have to figure out who this guy is and where this money is coming from. You never saw anything else suspicious? Anything that made you think the company wasn't on the up and up?"

I shake my head. "No, I've been there just over a year, and it all seemed great." I think back to all the interactions I had with Ricardo and the other employees, the company picnic on the beach, the lavish Christmas parties he hosted. "Looking back, maybe it was too good to be true. I got paid well. Huge cash bonuses. Had a boss who didn't want me working over-time or being there after hours. In retrospect, perhaps it should have raised some flags."

Viktoria holds up a hand. "It's okay. Don't beat yourself up over this. It isn't your fault."

"But it is." I blink away the tears welling in my eyes. "I should have known something was wrong before. Amelia would be alive if I hadn't been so naïve."

"Oh, honey." Viktoria approaches and sits on the side of the chair, wrapping her arm around my shoulders. "Don't blame yourself. It absolutely is *not* your fault. You can't think like that. What we need to concentrate on now is not placing blame but keeping you safe."

Kalen pushes off the counter and steps in front of me, squatting to get himself in my line of vision. Determination hardens his eyes. "We're not going to let anything happen to you."

Reaper nods. "I'm calling Preacher right now and filling him in on everything. He'll dig until he finds what we need." He looks at me. "Start writing down all the information you have so I can pass it along to him. Give me the video from your phone to send him, too. Maybe he can ID some of the guys from it."

Viktoria turns back to him. "I can ask Anya to help Preacher."

Reaper shakes his head. "No, there's no reason to get your sister involved in this right now. If we need her later, we can call her."

Turning back to me, Viktoria gives me a genuine smile. "I promise, everything's going to be okay."

It sure doesn't feel like it.

CHAOS

BY THE TIME Avery writes down all the information she knows off the top of her head and Reaper has spoken with Preacher, Avery is completely wrecked and can barely keep her eyes open. Her lids flutter as she talks with Viktoria, and the former cop tosses me a concerned look. She noticed it, too, and the way Reaper and Mouth are both eyeing me, it's time to let her get some much-needed sleep.

Seeing her like this tugs at feelings I've kept buried deep inside since our split, the protective instinct that I can never turn off when it comes to her, even if we aren't together.

Avery is the last person who would ever complain about anything. All the times I pulled away from her, the months I put up walls between us and pushed aside all her efforts to reach me, she didn't ever voice her concerns in a way that put the blame on me. She took all the responsibility for what was happening between us and never attacked me with the truth. At least, not until that final day.

She would never say she's exhausted and ask

everyone to leave, but she looks dead on her feet. If I don't step in, she's going to crash—hard.

"Let's wrap this up." I spin my finger around. "Time to go, guys."

Reaper, Mouth, and Viktoria don't protest my call and make their way toward the front door.

Viktoria pauses and turns back to me, leaning in to whisper so Avery can't hear. "Be nice to her, Chaos. She's a mess. She needs your help and support, not you running off to blow up shit and potentially make things worse."

I scowl at her. "Don't tell me what Avery needs. You don't know a fucking thing about her or us."

"No." Vik shakes her head. "You're right. I don't. But I know what fear looks like and that girl is utterly terrified. Don't fuck it up."

She turns and follows Reaper and Mouth out and down the steps with promises to touch base after we get a few hours of rest and give Preacher time to work his magic.

If anyone can find something on the fucker behind all this, it's Preacher. There's a reason he was one of the top CIA assets during the war and often worked with Delta and other spec ops groups; the man can work miracles. And that's what we need now.

As it stands, I can't see a way out of this for Avery that won't end in a whole lot of bloodshed and her stuck in the middle of it. The cops will already be all over the bodies up at the diner, and with Avery's car there and her nowhere to be found, they'll be looking for her, too. Given what she saw at that warehouse—one of their own apparently in bed with her boss—law enforcement finding her might be just as dangerous as if the man responsible for all this does.

Scrubbing a hand over my face, I turn back toward Avery to find her curled up and almost asleep in the chair. I approach her slowly, not wanting to startle her the way the guys' knocking did earlier.

"Avery?" I squat next to the chair and watch her peaceful face twist slightly. "Babe, wake up."

"Hmm?" Her eyes flutter open and finally focus on me. "What?"

"You're not sleeping here on the chair." I rise to my feet and hold up my palm to help her up. "You're taking my room."

She stares at my outstretched hand for a moment, almost like she's afraid to touch it, and the memory of the little zing that zapped between us earlier resurfaces, heating my skin.

Fuck.

I force myself to pull back my hand and motion toward the door near the kitchen. She rises slowly from the chair and follows me, the bag from Viktoria in her grasp.

There was a time, not all that long ago, when heading to the bedroom with Avery would have had me hard as a fucking rock, anticipating what was to come, when we would lose ourselves in each other for hours or days. But that's as far from what's about to happen as we've become from each other.

Let the past stay there.

Revisiting anything—good or bad—will only complicate what I have to do...what *we* have to do to make sure Avery is safe. Staying detached is the only way to survive in this world, and that means keeping things the way they should be with her—*off* limits.

This situation is more convoluted than I ever imagined when I first got her call...and it's only going to get worse.

I flip on the light switch to my bedroom and shift to the side to allow her to enter, already anticipating how she will react. She never was one to hold back on what she thinks, and that apparently hasn't changed much since we parted ways.

Avery steps in, scans the room quickly, and turns back to me. "You don't have a bed?"

I glance at the mattress on the floor, in the exact same place and state it's been since I left the house we shared. "Don't need one."

She motions to it, her pink lips agape slightly. "That *can't* be comfortable."

Comfortable isn't anything I've worried about for a long damn time—not since I stopped sleeping with her warm body pressed against mine. I rest where I can, when I can—which isn't very often, but I don't intend to tell her that. Avery would just worry, like she always did, especially at the end.

And staring at the simple mattress on the old wooden floor, the juxtaposition to what we had when we were together looms large. The king-sized bed with the massive, tufted headboard straight out of *Better Homes and Gardens*. The luxurious mattress we sank into together each night. The super-soft, high thread-count sheets against our heated, sweaty skin. The decorative throw pillows placed precisely each morning when we woke. The comfort I still dream about when I actually *do* sleep.

It was what Avery wanted.

And whatever she wanted...she got.

At least for a while...

While I was able to give it to her...

I shrug, trying not to make a big deal about the way I've been living. It isn't any of her concern, and I don't want it to be. "It's fine."

She narrows her eyes on me, unconvinced, and I have to look away because even after all this time, the woman's penetrating assessments seem to see right through me to everything I try to hide.

Her hands propped on her hips, she twists her lips. "Where are you going to sleep?"

"I'll take the chair."

"What?" She shakes her head, eyes wide. "No. You can't do that. You'll never get any rest on that thing. It's ancient and practically falling apart."

I lean toward her slightly, my retort slipping from my lips before I can bite it back. "I've slept in some pretty shitty places in my life. I'll be fine."

She stiffens slightly at the not-so-gentle reminder

of where I've been and what I've done. Even though I was never allowed to tell her the specifics of my missions, she knows enough that she understands exactly what I'm referring to now.

Maybe it was a low blow, one I shouldn't have made when she's already so on edge and suffering, but I need her to remember who and what I am. I can't have her thinking I'm the old Kalen, the one she knew *before*. Even hearing her call me Kalen instead of Chaos makes me simultaneously cringe and long for the past we can never go back to.

Avery can't confuse who we are now for who we were then, no matter how easy it might be to slip into old habits.

She takes a moment to recompose herself after my outburst and glances into the bag in her hand that Viktoria brought for her. "No pajamas."

Oh, hell.

Of course, not...

It's one blow after another—memory after memory.

I make my way over to my footlocker against the wall under the high, small window, tug it open, and grab one of my T-shirts. My fingers curl around the soft green material, and I pause for a moment, staring down at all my possessions—the only things I took with me when we split.

Avery's smile taunts me from the photo on top of the stack of clothes. In her white dress, veil tucked into her dark hair, the memory of how her lips pressed to mine felt after we said *I do* washes over me.

No.

I tighten my grip on the shirt and push the photo into the pile of shirts to keep it hidden, where it belongs. It shouldn't be there anyway. I should have thrown it away the day she served me the divorce papers. I should have destroyed every reminder of her. And I tried, but that photo saved me more times than I could count over the years, and I couldn't bear to throw it away along with the life we shared together.

Clearing my throat of the emotion suddenly clogging it, I walk over to Avery and hold out the shirt to her. "Here."

She stares at it for a long minute—long enough that I know exactly what she's thinking.

It's impossible to forget.

No matter how hard I might try.

The way the oversized material swam around her. The soft hem hitting her thighs just low enough to cover the parts I always wanted to see.

She loved sleeping in my shirts. The way it wrapped her in my scent when I was on deployment. Even when I was home, I couldn't get her to wear anything else to bed.

We stare at each other for what feels like hours. Neither one of us says anything about the situation to acknowledge how awkward or painful it is, and finally, she reaches out and takes it from me, offering me a little half smile.

"Thank you."

I incline my head and make my way back out toward the living room before either of us says or does something we'll regret later.

"Kalen?"

Shit.

I freeze and squeeze my eyes closed for a moment before opening them and turning back to face her. "Yeah?"

"Thank you...for everything. You didn't have to do this..." She trails off and averts her gaze for a second. "After...you know..." Her eyes flick up to meet mine again. "Everything."

Christ, she doesn't get it at all.

"Yeah, Avery, I did."

I leave it at that and let her close the door behind me. The latch clicking into place makes me fist my hands at my sides until they hurt, and I grab another beer, pop it open, and down half of it in one large gulp.

Something tells me I'm going to need a lot more of these before this situation is resolved. Hopefully, Preacher has some luck with the information we sent him and the video off Avery's phone.

Once we know who we're dealing with, we can form a solid plan—one that ends with eliminating all the threats and Avery right back where she belongs...

Living in bliss, somewhere far away from this mess or any I could create.

She deserves to be happy.

She deserves to have everything.

She deserves the world.

I was once stupid enough to think I could be the one to give it to her, too, but I'm older and wiser now and know what needs to happen.

That woman needs protection, and then she needs to get the fuck away from me.

6

AVERY

Bright light streaming in the west-facing window forces my eyes open, and I shift on the mattress, turning my head away and trying to bury it under the single pillow Kalen has in this place. All the tense and awkward moments we had last night and this morning before I finally crashed out and gave in to the sheer exhaustion my body was feeling float through my head.

Even after all this time, it's still there—that buzz of electricity, that attraction that draws us together. Only now, it's tangled up with so much pain and so many unspoken words that I can't even separate it anymore.

It's one tangled mass of messed-up, just like the man whose bed I'm lying in. There's a reason they call him Chaos, and being back in his orbit keeps reminding me of it. He works his way in and then destroys everything on his way out. That was what he did to me, to us. It just took a lot longer than it does with his usual targets.

But if I dwell on it, on what happened between us, I can't concentrate on what's important right now—figuring a way out of this situation Gramps would have called FUBAR.

If there even is one.

Kalen, Viktoria, and the guys keep telling me things will be okay, but their promises feel empty when we're facing such a huge unknown—and one apparently willing to kill to protect what's been happening right under my nose.

I just have to believe they're right and try to latch on to some of their conviction about the outcome because I don't have any of my own.

Given how high the sun is, I've slept for a while—though I'm confident Kalen hasn't. He never did sleep much after his first mission with Delta, never really relaxed enough to close his eyes and drift off. And he never would tell me why—either because he couldn't or wouldn't. Toward the end, after he got shot and almost died, he wouldn't even lie in the same bed with me.

And if I stay here any longer, wrapped up in his scent, the painful memories will only get more and more vivid. Yet, I still find myself bringing the T-shirt he gave me to my nose and inhaling deeply—taking in the familiar rich, leathery, masculine scent that's all Kalen.

The bedroom door opens before I can bring the fabric away from my face, and Kalen's eyes zero in on me like a missile, intent on destruction.

I jerk my hand away, even though it's far too late, and I've been caught by a man who never misses a single fucking detail. "How did you know I was awake?"

He shrugs nonchalantly, mug in one hand and a bag dangling from the other. "I just did."

The man could probably hear me shifting on this mattress from out there—one of the many super-human skills he's honed over the years. Or maybe he's just still that connected to me, still able to sense me from another room like he always seemed to be able to when we were married.

"Thought you could use some coffee." He holds up the cup. "Cream, three sugars."

I push myself to a sitting position, my back to the wall. "You remember how I take my coffee?"

He shifts uneasily on his feet, averting his gaze to the window. "It's not something you forget as many times as I made it for you."

"Right." I offer a tight smile, unsure if he's complaining about it or relishing the memory of him bringing it to me every morning and climbing into bed to share it the way I do. "Of course."

There are some things you can never forget about someone you love as much as I did Kalen, but the fact that he remembered that about me after all this time makes something warm and equally dangerous bloom in my chest.

He watches me, waiting for me to make some move.

I force a smile I'm not quite feeling. "Thank you. I'd love some coffee."

It might help wake me up and offer a replacement for Kalen's scent. I shift to the side, push off the cheap sheets and comforter, and rise from the mattress. Kalen's gaze drifts down to my bare legs—his T-shirt barely reaching the tops of my thighs. My skin sizzles with his assessment, the same way he always used to look at me when I was dressed like this. Something about seeing me in his shirts always drove him wild, and we'd end up fucking against a wall or tumble back into bed for another round.

But that was a long time ago.

"Give me a second to get my jeans back on."

He stands stock still for a moment, his gaze locked on my legs and slowly drifting up before he finally clears his throat and steps back. "Yeah." He holds out a bag dangling from his other hand. "Viktoria brought you the things you requested."

"Thanks." I accept it and the cup of coffee. "I'll probably take a shower, then."

He considers me for a moment, crossing his arms over his chest. The man always could read me like an open book. There isn't any way he won't sense my distress over the entire situation, which has only been exacerbated by having to come to *him* for help. "You okay?"

Am I okay?

"Jesus, Kalen"—I shake my head at his absurd question—"someone's trying to kill me. What do you think?"

I really wish I knew.

If I had been able to read him as well as he did me back when we were married, maybe I could have made things work, figured out a way to reach him when he was pushing me away. I might have found a way to make him stay.

He watches me for a minute without responding and takes a half-step toward me—one that sends butterflies racing through my stomach. His hand rises quickly, capturing my cheek in his calloused, rough palm before I can step back. He tightens his grip on my face, urging my eyes up to forcibly meet his. Conviction blazes there, mixed with a dark intensity I've never seen before, the thing that makes him Chaos.

"I'll make sure you're safe, Avery. You know that, right?"

The tenor of his words and touch sends a sense of calm rolling through me that I haven't felt since the moment I saw what I did in that warehouse.

His thumb brushes across my cheek. "Do you, Avery? Do you understand what I will do to protect you? The lengths I will go to?"

I nod slowly, unable to form words.

A low growl rumbles in his chest. "Good."

His hand abruptly falls away from my face, and he turns sharply on his heel, stalking away and pulling the door closed behind him.

I release a heavy breath, and my hand holding the coffee shakes so badly that the hot liquid splashes over the side onto my skin, shocking me back to the moment.

"Shit."

That man always knew how to unnerve me, and he does it even better now.

I take a sip of the coffee.

Perfect. Just like I knew it would be.

Kalen always made it exactly how I liked it and woke me the best way possible more often than I can count—with his face between my thighs and a hot cup waiting on the nightstand when I could finally breathe again.

Maybe a shower will help rid me of these memories.

If I'm lucky...

I make my way to the bathroom on the other side of the room and find it just as barren as the rest of the apartment—nothing personal aside from a toothbrush and some basic essentials.

Kalen spent a long time living out of a single bag with only what he absolutely needed. Even when he was home, he never kept more than this. Never anything but what he could pack in thirty seconds and become a ghost with.

He certainly acted like one, even with me at the end.

I take a few more sips, letting the warm liquid and

caffeine course through me before I strip. The bag Viktoria brought me contains everything I asked for. A few small things that might tide me over until I can get back to my apartment.

If I can get back...

A cold shiver rolls through me at that thought, but I shrug it off and grab the shampoo, conditioner, and soap. Hopefully, getting cleaned up will help me feel a little bit better, but no amount of scalding-hot water is going to wash away the tension between Kalen and me.

Nothing ever could.

Only my growling stomach eventually pulls me from the shower ten minutes later in search of food. I dress in the black yoga pants and T-shirt Viktoria brought and grab my now-cold cup of joe on my way out to the living room.

Viktoria stands at the counter, waiting for me, eyebrow raised. "Good morning."

"What are you doing here?" I scan the small space, but if Kalen were here, I'd know. Not only is there nowhere for him to hide, but whenever he's within ten feet of me, my heart and body tell me he's close. "Where's Kalen?"

"He left with the guys."

My stomach drops, and though I try my best to hide my reaction, Viktoria clearly sees my distress.

She raises her hand. "Don't worry, hon. I'm just as good with a gun as they are. I got you."

That wasn't the reason for the sudden sense of dread.

But I won't admit that to her.

"Where did he go?"

"They went to look into some of the initial information Preacher found."

"But what if—"

"They'll be all right. Those boys can take care of themselves."

They certainly can, but that never helped me worry any less that Kalen may not come home alive from his deployments. Others didn't. And while I got him back, he was never the same man. Each time he returned, it got worse and worse. Eventually, he wasn't Kalen at all.

God only knows what the years we've spent apart have continued to do to him mentally.

My stomach rumbles loudly, drawing Viktoria's sharp gaze.

"God, when was the last time you ate, hon?"

Was it really only yesterday that all this started, that I found that zip drive and sent my life into this fucking tailspin?

"Um, yesterday some time. Lunch, I guess?"

"Here." She slides a bag across the counter. "I brought some sandwiches because I assumed Chaos doesn't keep anything that's actually edible here."

Chaos wouldn't.

Kalen would have, though.

He was always so thoughtful, so caring, constantly making sure I had everything I needed or wanted, even if it meant running out in the middle of the night to get ice cream or anything else. The man spoiled me, then as soon as he saw me in one of his T-shirts, he would simply lift the hem and fuck me wherever we were, reminding me of how much he loved me and needed me.

In the kitchen...

On the bathroom counter...

Over the back of the couch...

My pussy clenches at the memory, and I squeeze on nothing and suck in a deep breath.

That was the old Kalen, the one who still wanted you. The one who promised he would never leave.

But he did.

This is who you have now, Avery.

This is what's left.

Chaos...

But Chaos is definitely the right one for the job and probably a lot safer for my heart.

CHAOS

"So"—REAPER drawls—"we're not going to talk about it?"

I glance over at him in the driver's seat and scowl. "Talk about what?"

He raises an eyebrow at me and glances my way before returning his focus to the road. "The fact that your ex-wife is at your place, who you haven't talked to in, what, five years?"

"Four years...and there's nothing to talk about."

Mouth barks a laugh from the backseat, and I twist around to offer him the same glare I just did Reaper.

"What the hell are you laughing at?"

He holds up his hands innocently and grins.

I settle back into my seat, arms crossed over my chest. "There's nothing to talk about. She needed help. I'm offering it. End. Of. Story."

Reaper snorts. "Sure, just like I was only protecting Viktoria because I didn't want her to get caught up in the middle of my mission against Yankovich."

"Definitely not the same thing."

He shakes his head, chuckling under his breath. "Whatever you say, man. You want to sit there and pretend like having that woman in your place isn't really fucking with you? You go right ahead. Just make sure it doesn't affect your ability to maintain your focus when we do what we need to do."

I grit my teeth to stop myself from launching across the center console and giving Reaper the beating he deserves for that comment. "I'm fucking good, Reaper."

His shoulders rise and fall. "Good."

I stare out at the road in front of us, busy with mid-day traffic. "Where are we headed, anyway?"

All Reaper said before they picked me up today was we were meeting up for recon, but he never said where or of what.

He inclines his head toward a sheet of paper on the dashboard. "We're going to the first place on the list Avery gave us of the various holdings of Ricardo Perez. Avery said he seems to spend a lot of time at a restaurant he owns called *South of the Border*. It looks like it's only a few miles away from the headquarters and warehouse where she worked and saw the body of her co-worker."

"Let's hit it first, see if we can find out why he's spending so much time there. We can swing over to the warehouse later. Right now, we need to get the lay of the land a little bit."

Preacher hasn't been able to come up with much yet beyond what Avery was able to give him last night, but we have a few locations to check out while he keeps doing whatever it is he does behind that wall of computers to find information that seems impossible for anyone else to locate.

Reaper glances at me briefly. "What are you thinking?"

I shrug. "It seems as though this Ricardo guy is either laundering funds through his businesses or trafficking drugs, perhaps both. Could be connected to one of the cartels."

He nods. "It's possible. More than likely, actually. It would explain how and why they so easily took out her friend when she started to get suspicious. They can't have anyone nosing around who might interfere with what they're doing."

I swallow thickly. "Or witness any of their crimes." The words taste like acid on my tongue because I know what that means for Avery.

She's gotten herself into a completely fucked-up situation that will likely take a lot of bloodshed to fix.

"That man sent a *hit* squad after her, for fuck's sake. Whatever he's hiding, it's big, and he wants it to stay hidden."

Mouth's large hand lands on my shoulder and squeezes, silently letting me know he's with me and will protect Avery with everything he has in him. I reach up and pat his fingers, thanking him without words because my throat suddenly feels too tight to speak again.

What I told Reaper was a lie.

I'm not good.

Far from it.

Avery was my entire world for so long, and then...it was over so fast, I didn't even have a chance to look back before she was gone. I never thought I'd see her again, never thought I'd feel her touch, yet my palm still tingles from where it cupped her cheek this morning, her familiar, smooth, soft skin against my abrasive, gnarled fingertips.

Get it out of your head.

I need to be *crystal* clear going into this, or things will go sideways fast.

Reaper takes a left down Fleet Street toward *South of the Border*. The restaurant sign comes into view two blocks down, and he pulls into a lot for an empty building across the street and throws the car into park.

We all stare at the business for a moment. A few cars dot the parking lot and indicate that it has some customers. From the outside, it looks completely legitimate. Exactly as Perez likely designed it.

Reaper flips open his lighter and flicks it closed again, the repetitive sound somehow soothing after all these years of hearing it. "Do you think it's a good idea? Showing our faces in there."

I shrug. "They're not going to know us from Adam. We're just three dudes looking for some good Mexican food. That's all they are ever going to know."

We watch the place for another hour to two, waiting for anything suspicious to happen, but when all remains quiet, Reaper eventually sighs, shoves his lighter back into his pocket, then throws the car into drive and crosses the street to the *South of the Border* lot.

The spot in front of the main doors is open, and he pulls in and parks with a wink at me. "Right by the front doors to make a quick getaway."

"If we need to make a quick getaway, then we're doing something wrong."

Mouth barks out another laugh, and we all climb from the car to make our way into the restaurant casually, ignoring the four exterior cameras I count on the outside of the building facing the front lot.

A bell above the door jingles.

We each scan around us, taking in every detail of the space and everyone in it while making our way toward the front counter.

The teenage boy at the register. An older man staffing the kitchen in the back. The couple in front of him ordering—the man with his arm around the shorter woman's shoulders. A second couple at a table in the corner talking in hushed tones, holding hands across empty plates.

We step into line behind the couple at the counter, and as inconspicuously as possible, I count the interior cameras. Three facing the registers, three facing out into the dining room. One facing down a hallway to the right, likely leading to the kitchen entrance and bathrooms.

Reaper scans the menu on the wall above and behind the teen, mumbling something to Mouth, who nods. I check it out and determine my order while watching the old man through the open service window to the kitchen.

Only two employees...

Odd.

This place isn't exactly bustling, but one would think they need more than two people working here, especially near dinner time.

The couple in front of us steps to the side, and Reaper shifts up against the counter and nods at the young kid.

"Hey, man, can I get six tacos—three *al pastor*, three *lengua*, and whenever these two assholes want."

A grin spreads across the teen's face, already at ease with us based on Reaper's description.

I scowl at my best friend and incline my head toward the kid. "I'll have the same, and this guy"—I motion toward Mouth—"will have three *al pastor* and three *carne asada*."

Mouth grunts his agreement, and the teen rings it

up and gives Reaper the total. Reaper pays, and the couple from the table rises to drop off their empty plates in the trash and make their way out toward a beat-up pickup in the lot, leaving us with the two employees and the couple waiting for their food near the end of the counter.

Reaper leans against the wall next to me and crosses one ankle over the other, his arms folded across his chest. "So, what's going on with you two?"

I scowl at him. "We're really getting into this again?"

He shrugs. "What else we got to talk about?"

"She's my ex-wife. That *ex* is for a reason."

"Yeah"—he nods slowly—"you never *did* tell us what that reason was, you know, just said she served you with papers when you got home from that mission."

"I didn't tell you because what happened between us is *our* business."

"Was it money business or fucking business?"

My hands fist at my sides and only Mouth's firm grip on my shoulder keeps me from decking Reaper.

Reaper's dark eyebrows wing up, and he holds up his hands in surrender. "Wow. Aren't we a bit testy?"

"I don't ask you about your sex life with Viktoria."

He shakes his head. "No, you just watched us have sex in the damn shower."

I release a hard laugh that draws the attention of the couple waiting who just steps away. "To be fair, you knew we were coming and invited us there. So..."

"So, you could have waited in the goddamn living room."

I shrug it off and give him a little half grin. "What fun would that have been?"

"Yeah, yeah."

He isn't seriously mad about it; though, he would have every right to be—unless you're into that kind of shit. Watching your buddy bang his woman isn't the type of thing we usually get into so that was a special occasion.

The old man from the kitchen hands a bag through the window to the teen, who brings it forward to the front counter for the couple next to us. They grab it and make their way out, the bell over the door jingling.

With their departure, the old man returns to cooking and the teenager at the register fumbles around on his cell phone.

Reaper glances at me. "You know, it wouldn't be so bad if you just hooked back up with your wife."

I scowl at him. "Leave it the fuck alone, Reaper."

"We know what's good for you."

We?

I glance at Mouth and raise an eyebrow. "Oh, you're in on this, too?"

He offers a half-smile and shrugs. I'd give anything to hear one of his wisecracks and completely inappropriate comments right now. We could all use a good laugh. Instead, he just leans his shoulder against the wall and watches for our food.

The old man slides three trays across the order

window, and the teen grabs each one and passes them to the edge of the counter.

Reaper grabs his and smiles at the kid. "Thanks, man." He scans the restaurant. "Hey, we've never been here before. Do your parents own this place or something?"

He shakes his head. "No, my uncle does." He points a skinny finger to the old man in the back. "That's my grandpa."

"Ah." Reaper nods. "Gotcha. Well, everything looks great."

We all grab our trays and make our way to one of the empty tables in the center of the restaurant, where one of us can watch the parking lot while the other two keep an eye on Ricardo's employees.

Keeping it all in the family, apparently.

The aroma of the grilled meats and various spices waft up to my nose, and my stomach growls. I didn't realize how hungry I was until this moment. All I've been thinking about is Avery and how best to protect her. I could have gone days without eating, worrying about that, if keeping *her* safe didn't require me to come here and actually fucking eat.

I dig into the surprisingly decent food. It goes down easily as we watch various people come in and out of the restaurant occasionally—most ordering food to go.

Halfway through my tacos, I wipe my mouth and clear my throat. "I'm gonna hit the head."

Mouth and Reaper nod their understanding, and I casually walk to the hallway that runs along the side of the restaurant. The kid at the register doesn't even look up from his phone as I pass him and make my way down—past the women's bathroom, past the men's bathroom, to the closed door on my right.

I twist the knob, find it unlocked, and push it open.

Cleaning supplies.

Another two feet down the hall, the entrance to the kitchen gives me a view of the old man bent over the flat top, humming to himself softly. The rest of the cooking area appears uninteresting. It could use a good cleaning, but otherwise, nothing suspicious.

Until my eyes land on a closed door along the back wall.

Why the hell would an office in a place like this need biometric locks and security knobs?

It doesn't make any sense, especially since *South of the Border* doesn't seem very busy. Most restaurants keep a small safe in the office. Nothing as extravagant as this setup would be necessary for that.

I poke my head into the kitchen and glance around for cameras.

There aren't any back here—not in the kitchen, not near the rear entrance to the restaurant, not near *this* door. They don't want anything that goes on inside *here* filmed. They just want to be able to see what happens on the outside of the building and in the restaurant itself. See who's coming.

Who the fuck are these people, and what the hell are they going to do to Avery if they find her?

7

_____

AVERY

"Do you think they're okay?" My knee bounces rapidly, the constant motion somehow helping me from completely losing my mind as the minutes and hours tick by. "They've been gone a long time."

Viktoria looks at me from her spot perched on the small kitchen counter, her legs dangling beneath her, and chuckles. "You do know what they do, right?" One of her dark eyebrows rises. "You know what they're capable of?"

I swallow back the bile rising in my throat and give her a little half-nod. "Yeah. I mean"—I shake my head—"I'm pretty sure I do. None of them would have ever made Delta if they weren't the best, right?"

She offers a half-shrug and slides off the counter with a sigh. "They know what they're doing, Avery. If anyone is going to be able to sort out the situation, it's those three."

I take a deep breath and try to calm my heart which has only seemed to race more and more the longer they're gone. The uncertainty is liable to give me a coronary or eat a hole through my stomach— maybe both. "I hope you're right."

Viktoria drums her fingers on the counter, the sound mixing with the noise coming from the television neither of us is really watching. She glances at me out of the corner of her eye, her assessment burning a hole in my cheek, like if she looks hard enough, she might find what she's searching for. "What happened between you two?"

"What?"

"What happened between you and Chaos? Why did you get divorced?" She shakes her head with a wistful look. "The way you two look at each other..."

She trails off, and I wince at the observation she's so easily made after only seeing us together for a short time.

"I wish I could explain it."

I wish I understood it.

When we were young, I thought I *did* understand it. I thought I understood *him.* I thought we were an unbreakable team, but in the end, he chose another team, another relationship over ours.

Vik leans back against the counter and crosses her arms over her chest. "Try."

Sighing, I lie back in the recliner, staring at the off-white ceiling with the dried water stains. "I don't know. We were high school sweethearts, dated junior and senior year. Got married right after. We were young, but things were really good. I knew he had planned to enlist out of high school. It was *always* the plan. He loved it. And I was actually happy being an army wife for a while."

"For a while?"

I glance over at her. "Things changed when he went to Delta." Just saying those words makes a vise tighten around my chest. "It's all he ever wanted, what he worked toward. He loved being a Ranger, but he wanted Delta. So, I was happy for him, for us, but whatever they were doing, it just..." I shake my head, thinking back to those first few assignments. "He came back different than he was—still Kalen, but he brought Chaos back with him."

Admitting that out loud to anyone for the first time feels both like a giant weight off my shoulders and a crushing blow to the gut at the same time.

"I always knew he had a special talent that couldn't be wasted. I knew he was doing it to protect our country, protect us, and to help innocent people in really shitty situations. I never had any problem with it. Until he started cutting me out."

Vik's gaze softens. "What do you mean?"

I shrug. "He had things he could never tell me. I understood that. But we stopped talking about anything that wasn't small talk you have with a loose acquaintance, and then, after the team lost Mayhem and he and Mouth got hurt, it all changed even more."

Viktoria nodded slowly. "I've heard bits and pieces of it, but obviously, it's not something they can talk about in detail."

"I got the call that he'd been hurt." Tears finally trickle down my cheeks. "I fucking panicked. I thought I was going to lose him. They said he had lost a lot of blood, that they had to give him several transfusions, that they weren't sure he was going to make it. By the time they got him Stateside and I could actually see him, he was doing a little bit better. But he wouldn't even look me in the eye. He barely acknowledged me when I went into the hospital room. He didn't want me there, had the nurses urge me out."

The pain of those moments strikes me hard, knocking the air from my lungs. I try to take a shaky deep breath but only manage a shallow, sharp one.

"It was like a switch had flipped, and he went from warm and caring to icy cold with me. He came home and wouldn't even sleep in the same bed. He slept in this chair until I finally served divorce papers on him when he came back from his next mission."

"Wow." Vik nods slowly, trying to absorb it all. "That's pretty heavy. Why didn't you to try to work it out? Couples counseling or something? Like I said, I've seen the way you two look at each other."

I shake my head. "It wouldn't have mattered. He never would have gone to counseling. He never would have talked about it with a stranger if he wouldn't even talk about it with me. All he wanted to do was be with the boys, to be with his team. The people who understood what he was going through." A sob slips from my mouth, and I press my hand over it. "He-he didn't love me anymore."

Her sharp bark of laughter startles me upright. "I think you're wrong on that, Avery."

Tears stream down my cheeks unbidden now, and I shake my head. "No, I'm not. What you see is the same attraction that's always been there. It probably always will be. Sex was never our problem. When he came back, we had sex a lot. And I mean *a lot*. But it was like he was trying to fuck his way out of whatever memory was haunting him so badly, and then he would leave me to sleep by myself while he went out to our living room to sleep on this damn chair."

I shove away from the offending piece of furniture with a huff, even though it isn't the recliner's fault. Viktoria watches me pace the room, remaining quiet, letting me think my way through the swirl of memories and emotions threatening to suffocate me right now.

"I'm just..." I shake my head, not able to make sense of anything any more now than I could back then. "I don't know. I can't tell you what happened. I really can't."

Our life together was beautiful. It was perfect. It was what we always dreamed it would be. And then, it just...wasn't anymore.

I've never tried to explain it to anyone before, only ever mulled it over endlessly in my own head, going over every second, every minute, every hour of every day of every year we spent together to try to figure out *where* and *how* it went wrong.

Four years haven't given me any more insight into it.

I stop pacing and face Viktoria, offering one final shrug as a period at the end of my explanation. "He just...blew everything apart, but that's what he's always been good at, so I guess I should have seen it coming. I should have expected Chaos would eventually touch us, and it did more than that. It destroyed everything."

CHAOS

THE ASSHOLE after Avery has no idea we're on to him and his operation. He has no fucking clue who he's up against. Of all the women in the world to go after, he chose the wrong fucking one, and now, he'll face Chaos as a consequence.

We park in the lot diagonally across the street from the restaurant, waiting for it to completely clear out for the night. The old man leaves first, then the younger teenage boy, carrying a bag of garbage to toss into the dumpster before he climbs into his rickety car and heads home.

Time ticks by slowly as we watch for something, anything, but the building remains dark and empty.

I glance at my watch again. "Almost two. Whatever's happening in that back room has to be after hours, or they do a damn good job of keeping it under wraps if it's happening while they're open."

"What do you think?" Reaper inclines his head toward the place. "It's been an hour since the teenager left, and there's been no movement."

Whatever Perez has going on in that place, it isn't happening tonight, which makes it the perfect time to go in. "Let's go."

Reaper and I climb from the car with our weapons and my bag the guys packed before they picked me up earlier, and he signals to Mouth, where he already waits on the roof of the building next to our car. From that vantage point, he can watch every move and alert us if anyone's coming—and take out any potential threats before they can get to us.

We aren't taking any chances with this guy, not after we know he killed an innocent woman and tried to take out Avery. It isn't a question of *if* he's dangerous but simply a level of degree. And something tells me, with this guy, it's very high.

Mouth signals back from the roof, and we make our way across the street toward *South of the Border*, staying out of sight of the exterior cameras they so meticulously placed. Once we reach the pole that leads to the electrical box for the restaurant, we access it and prepare to cut the power.

We'll have five minutes—seven tops—before the security company alerts them or someone shows up here to check out what's happening.

We won't need that long.

Not even close.

Reaper snips the wire as I set the timer on my watch, and we race across the back parking lot to the rear door, which jimmies open easily without the assistance of the electronic locks on the interior door. We step inside, utilizing our night vision googles so we don't need to turn on any lights to see.

The eerie silence of the place envelops us, and we quickly move through, clearing the restaurant and kitchen before we approach the heavily secured door at the back.

I signal to Reaper that I'm moving in and kneel to set the charge on the electronic box, which unfortunately has a battery backup keeping it locked even though we cut the power.

This charge should take care of it. Just enough to get the door open. Not loud enough to alert any neighboring businesses that anything's wrong.

We don't waste any time moving behind the cook line and detonating the device. The explosion slightly rumbles the floor, and smoke begins to fill the kitchen, but it did the trick. The destroyed door pushes open easily, and we quickly clear the room.

No windows—no other way in or out.

And no sign of anyone inside.

I pull out a chemlight and crack it, illuminating the space with a greenish hue. We push our night vision goggles up and examine the room.

Bankers' boxes stacked ten high line each wall,

and a row of metal tables runs up the center, littered with bill counters, rubber bands, and paper bill wraps.

A whiteboard on the side wall lists staggering numbers that must be incoming funds, and when I pull the lid off the top of one of the boxes, the cash is stacked so tightly that there isn't any room for even a single one more.

If all these boxes are full, there's a fuckload of money in this tiny room.

Which means a fuckload of trouble.

Reaper motions toward all of it. "You think they're laundering for the cartel?"

"It would make sense. Most of these restaurants are cash businesses. Same with a lot of the deliveries they make."

"You think they're dealing out of here, too?"

I shake my head. "If they are, they're not packaging here. No scales, no baggies. No residue on the tables. And I can't see gramps and the nephew doing that, either."

Reaper nods his agreement. "So, what do you want to do?"

I glower at him. "What the fuck do you *think* I want to do?"

The tiniest grin pulls at Reaper's lips. "Burn the place to the fucking ground."

"Damn fucking straight."

There isn't any other option. If we sit idly by and let Perez continue with what he's been doing, he'll keep coming after Avery, and other innocent people will get hurt.

I reach into my bag and pull out the charges I prepared before we came, placing one on each wall before I step out into the restaurant and secure three more at the exact locations I know will create the most damage.

My radio crackles—three clicks followed by a single one.

Mouth's signal that someone's coming.

"We've got company."

Reaper touches my arm. "You sure you don't want to just let the police come in and find all this evidence?"

I issue a low growl. "So that fucker can claim he knew nothing about it, that it was his men or the sweet old grandfather or nephew working here? So he can walk away scot-fucking-free? No fucking way, man."

Reaper shrugs. "I figured, but I thought I should ask."

"This is what we do, isn't it? Exact our own methods of justice?"

"What will justice be in this situation?"

We make it to the back door, and I pause for a second and lock gazes with Reaper. "When I have my hands around this fucker's throat and watch him take his last breath as I squeeze it from him. After I've already taken everything he cherishes and loves, every-thing he's worked so hard for. Then, I'll be satisfied because then, I'll know Avery is safe."

Until then, I'll just keep blowing up whatever gets in my way.

I step out into the night with Reaper hot on my heels, and we hoof it toward the car. Mouth jumps from the fire escape of the building next to us and jogs over to join us, rifle in hand. We pile in and pull away, and I turn back to watch the building as I detonate the charges.

The blast shakes the car and rumbles the ground like an earthquake. Fireballs erupt into the night sky, orange and red columns of flame that feel like seeing what victory actually looks like.

Reaper glances back in the rearview mirror. "How much money do you think was in there?"

I shrug. "I don't know. Three million? Maybe four?"

However much it was, it's going to put a dent in Perez's business and may give him something else to focus on besides Avery long enough for me to kill the motherfucker.

8

_____

CHAOS

The silent ride back from the rubble that is now *South of the Border* gives me far too much time to think about what I must face when I get home.

I used to relish returning from a mission to Avery waiting for me, used to fantasize about what I would do to her when I finally had her in my arms again. I would wipe away all the turmoil in my soul by driving into her welcoming body and accepting her loving touch.

But that's not what will be waiting for me tonight.

Avery is a broken woman with a target on her back who needed my help.

Nothing more.

She isn't my wife.

She isn't my anything.

We pull into the driveway of the repair shop, and Reaper reaches out and grabs my arm, stopping me from climbing from the car.

"Tonight was a good start. We got this."

I incline my head in agreement to him and Mouth, then head toward the side of the building and the stairs leading to my apartment a little slower than I normally might, a part of me dreading what might happen when I walk inside again.

The door to my apartment opens before I even make it halfway up the steps, and if we hadn't already called ahead and told Vik we were on our way back, I might have pulled my weapon, concerned about who might be coming out. As it stands, I'm glad someone was able to stay with Avery and watch her while I was otherwise occupied. Vik and I may butt heads at times, but without her here, we would have had to call in Flash or Cutter or one of the other guys who are in the country to assist, and we don't have the time to wait for anyone else to get here to act. Not with Avery's life on the line.

Viktoria slips out and gently eases the door closed behind her with a tiny wince at the noise it makes. I stop on the small landing just outside my place, and she leans back against the door, blocking my path, and gives me a look that could kill.

It isn't anything new from Vik, but concern for Avery trumps my raised hackles at Reaper's woman's attitude toward me.

"What? Is she okay?"

"Really?" Vik rolls her eyes and motions behind her. "She's scared out of her fucking mind. She's confused being this close to you again. And she barely ate—"

"I'll get her to eat."

She snorts and shakes her head with a humorless sigh. "Good luck with that, Chaos. I don't know why men always think they can get women to do whatever they tell them to."

"Because we usually know what's best."

"Wow." Her jaw falls open. "Is *that* why you destroyed that girl? Because you thought that was what was best?"

Her words knock me back a step, but I do my best to hide my reaction from the woman who loves to needle me about everything like she's one of the guys.

Destroyed her?

"Is that what Avery said I did?"

Did I destroy the woman who was my everything?

Viktoria looks over the railing down at the car where Reaper sits waiting for her. "Not in those words, but it's obvious, Chaos. She's a mess, and not just because of what she saw or because she's in danger. That girl is worried about her heart as much as she is her life." She releases a heavy sigh and returns her focus to me, her normally hard gaze softening for a moment. "I finally forced her to go lie down and get some sleep."

"I'll be quiet when I go in."

I take a step to move around her to the door, and she places her hand against my chest firmly.

"Don't mess around with that woman's heart. I don't think she can take it."

Me either.

She releases me, hustles down the steps, and climbs into the car with Reaper. They pull away, and I wait until their tail lights disappear down the tree-lined street before I open the door quietly and secure the deadbolt and chain behind me. Leaning back against the closed door, I inhale a long, deep breath.

Big mistake.

It smells like her.

Even though she's only been here a day, her light, flowery scent permeates everything. I'll probably have to move once this is over and get rid of anything she touched, like the chair I trudge over to with plans to settle in it for the night.

I kick off my boots and start to lower myself down into it, but something draws me back to my feet and toward the bedroom. The door stands slightly ajar, and I nudge it open and step inside.

A bright trail of moonlight filters through the partially raised blinds and falls onto the mattress, where Avery lies, her back to me. Her fragile form makes my heart squeeze in my chest. It's the same one I looked forward to coming home to after every mission. Clinging to every night. The one that fits perfectly with mine. Like she completed me and made me whole.

My feet carry me to the far wall where my foot-locker sits, and I lower myself down next to it and lean back against the chipping-off white paint with a low sigh.

Tonight might feel like a victory—and in a way, it was. We learned something useful, and we hurt him by destroying all that cash and one of his places of business. But it doesn't solve the bigger problem, doesn't eliminate the threat to Avery.

The only way that will happen is if Ricardo Perez is gone.

This was only the tip of the iceberg. We have a lot of work ahead of us. A lot of death and destruction will have to happen before Avery is safe.

I scrub my hands over my face, rubbing at my tired eyes.

When was the last time I even slept?

Two days ago?

Three?

It doesn't really matter.

I've gone a lot longer on a lot less sleep, but never when anything so important was at stake. Not when my very heart is at risk. And I'd be kidding myself if I said this woman doesn't still hold it.

Sitting here, watching her sleep, so peaceful even with everything going on, my T-shirt wrapped around her, her beautiful face calm and serene, it makes my cock swell against the zipper of my jeans.

No other woman has done that to me since Avery, and none ever could. I belong to her mind, body, and soul and always will, even when we can't be together. Even when it's impossible.

Avery staying here like this will be torture, but it's the best place for her. Perhaps the only safe place she can go now.

She was once my safe place. I came home to her and felt her arms wrap around me, her body welcoming me, and I was able to forget everything that had happened during my missions. All the horrible actions I witnessed, the evil people I saw, and the things I had to do vanished. She was *safe*. Until suddenly, she wasn't. Until she became part of the greater nightmare.

AVERY

I STEP through the unlocked door near the loading docks into the warehouse, searching for Ricardo. Rushed, frustrated voices fill the air, making me tense and pause. I've never been here this late, but no one should be.

Something's wrong.

Inching around the large truck onto the main floor, Ricardo and several men finally come into view doing something near one of the freezers toward the back.

Loading a truck at this hour?

My gut churns immediately, knowing something isn't right. They shouldn't be here. This truck shouldn't be here. The information on the drive I left on my desk shouldn't exist.

This is wrong. All wrong.

Sweat beads across my forehead, and my hands start to shake at my sides as I step farther into the warehouse slowly.

Somehow, I know what's coming...but I still pull out my phone and record them.

I *know* what's coming...but I can't look away.

They pull open the walk-in freezer and drag out Amelia's bloodied body. Her open, dead, glazed-over eyes that once held so much life and joy stare at me. Her lips parted, begging me for help in a silent scream only I can hear.

My own cry wrenches from my throat and breaks through the air around me, piercing and frantic. The sound jolts me upright on the mattress, my heart thundering against my ribcage and blood rushing in my ears.

A sob falls from my lips, and tears pour down my cheeks like a tidal wave I can't stop.

"Avery..." Kalen's firm voice floats to me.

Probably just another dream...

Like what I just saw...

A dream that's also a memory...

One horrible...

One all I ever wanted...

"Avery, it's okay. I'm here." His voice gets louder. "You're safe."

The mattress dips, and familiar, strong arms wrap

around me and pull me against a solid chest I know so well. I bawl, clutching at the material that smells so much like him, feeling the steady beat of his heart under my palm.

"It was just a dream." His large hand rubs up and down my back slowly, the touch so soothing, it almost makes me forget for one minute why I'm here, and he buries his face in my hair, holding me tightly to him. "You're safe, babe. No one can get to you here. I promise."

Here.

Kalen's place.

The apartment above the garage.

I suck in a deep, shaky breath.

I'm not at the warehouse.

I'm not seeing her again.

I cling to him like he's my lifeline, like he's the only thing keeping me present, in the here and now. And he is. If not for him, I'd be dead by now. Perez's men would have caught up with me at the diner and finished what they tried to start when they were chasing me in the car.

Not so long ago, I thought Kalen's leaving had ended my life—at least, any form of it where I was happy and content—but now, he's the one keeping me alive, keeping me secure. In the worst moment of my life, he's the one *here*.

Kalen pulls me away slightly and stares down at me in the moonlight, brushing away my tears with his thumbs. "Are you okay?"

I try to take another deep breath, but it gets caught on another sob, no matter how hard I work to keep from falling apart. "No..." I shake my head, sniffling. "I don't know. I saw her again, Kalen. I saw what they did to her..."

He drags me back against him, settling me on his lap and squeezing me tightly again, cocooning me in his strength. "I'm so sorry you had to see that. No one should ever have to see anyone like that, let alone their friends."

His words slash at my heart like a knife, the true meaning behind them lying just beneath the surface. Kalen has watched so many of his friends get hurt, get killed. He might be one of the only people on Earth who understands how this feels.

And he's here.

He's back.

"What time is?"

Fingers trail up and down my spine soothingly. "Late, early, actually."

"What were you doing in here?"

He stiffens under me for a moment before his hands resume their movement and he tips his head toward the wall beside his footlocker. "Sitting."

"And...watching me sleep?"

"Thinking. Making sure you were okay." He shifts to take my face between his palms, forcing me to meet his gaze. "Are you, really? It's okay to say no. I would understand if you did."

I don't know how to respond or what to say. For the

first time in days, sitting here with him, enveloped in his arms, his strength, so close, I actually do feel all right for a second.

There's a flicker of hope that all this will go away, that I'll wake from it being a bad dream and go back to the days when he was my Kalen and not Chaos.

"No, I'm not okay." I manage to take a cleansing breath. "But I feel a lot better now that you're here."

He seems to consider my words for a moment before answering, like he's searching for some hidden meaning in them. "Viktoria can protect you. For me to do what I have to, I'm not going to be able to be here all the time. I wouldn't leave you with her if I wasn't confident that she will eliminate any threat."

"I know. I just..." I let my words trail off—unsure whether I should or maybe unwilling to say them.

"You just what?"

I press my hands against his strong chest and curl my fingers into the soft material. "It's just...having you here makes me feel safe. It always did."

His jaw hardens as he looks at me. "Don't, Avery." He shakes his head. "Please don't."

"Don't what?"

He shifts back slightly, then pulls me off his lap and sets me back onto the mattress before pushing to his feet, running his hands through his hair. "Don't put me in this position."

"What position?"

Instead of answering, he moves toward the open door, his body stiff.

"Kalen, please don't go."

He pauses with his back to me, shoulders rising and falling with his hard breaths.

"Stay with me."

The words hang in the air between us—heavy with so many things we never said to each other.

He stands frozen for a few minutes—minutes that seem like they'll never end, his hands opening and closing into fists at his sides. Finally, he slowly turns toward me, his jaw still clenched, body tense. "Avery..."

This time, my name comes out like a benediction, a prayer, something holy and unworthy for him to be speaking.

So much has happened between us. There are so many things we should be discussing, conversations he wouldn't have with me before that need to happen. But in this moment, all I want is to be in his arms again, for it to be the way it was before, to find a way to forget what's happening around us.

All I want is for him to give me *that*.

9

CHAOS

Avery looks at me like I'm the only person in the world who can give her what she needs right now, and I've never been able to deny her anything. Even when our relationship was falling apart, when *I* was falling apart, I couldn't stay away from her. I couldn't stop myself from touching her and loving her, giving her what she needed—at least physically. And now, she's asking for me to be there again, for me to be the one who gets her through this.

I don't know that I have the willpower to say no.

"Please, Kalen..." She stares at me with big green eyes, her bottom lip quivering, wrapped in my shirt, her hair rumpled, and looking so fucking broken and beautiful that my chest hurts.

"This isn't a good idea, Avery." I swallow thickly,

trying to find the right words to explain to her what she's really asking. "In fact, it's a very bad one."

Avery slowly climbs off the bed and approaches me, her long, bare legs glowing almost white in the moonlight coming from the window. "I don't care right now."

She stops in front of me and slowly presses her palm over my chest, unshed tears shimmering in her eyes from the dream she just had and maybe because she's afraid I'll say no.

My stomach twists, a jumbled mess of desire and restraint. "You're sure this is what you want, Avery? Really sure? Because if I don't walk out of here right now, it's going to happen."

It's the only warning I can give her. I've stayed away for years because I knew even just being in a room with her would be enough for me to lose control. Enough for me to snap and give in to how much I need her. How much I've always needed her even though I can't have her.

She leans closer to me, her lips only an inch from mine. "Yes, Kalen, I'm sure." Her fingers curl into my chest like she's grasping me to find some semblance of control over her life that seems to be spiraling. "Please..."

I can't have her. It's not good for either of us. Not safe for her.

But maybe for one night...

For *one night*, I can feel her in my arms again. Feel her underneath me. Feel her kiss and touch and give her what she needs.

And then everything can go back to the way it was. The way it *has* to be.

I can do this for her. I can give her this and live with the consequences of knowing what it feels like to be inside her again so she can find some peace in all this lunacy.

It doesn't matter how much it will hurt me tomorrow. She needs this.

I wrap my arms around her and drag her to me, crashing my lips to hers. A tiny mewl slips from her mouth, and she molds her body to mine, my cock hardening between us and pressing against her familiar, luscious curves.

She clings to me like she can't get close enough. Like she needs it and me more than anything else in this moment. Her lips move desperately against mine, seeking something, anything to take away her pain.

And selfishly, I'm going to give it to her.

Even though I should back away, even though I should walk out of this room and lock her in it for her own good, even though it's going to hurt later...

Despite all of it, I reach for the hem of my shirt hanging near her hips, tugging it up and hovering with it just below her breasts. "You know what it does to me to see you in this, don't you, Avery?"

My voice comes out gravelly, the heavy weight of what we're about to do making it hard to speak.

She ghosts her lips over mine. "I know."

The history between us doesn't stop me from

pulling the shirt over her head, exposing her bare breasts, taut stomach, and the tiny scrap of fabric barely covering her pussy.

"Jesus, Avery, you had Viktoria buy you thongs?"

A low growl rumbles in my chest as I drag her naked body up against mine and press my lips to hers again, devouring the woman I know so well and have spent so much time thinking about, dreaming about, worrying about, who is tangled in every good memory I have of my entire life since I met her at sixteen.

She wraps her arms around my neck and scratches her fingers across the skin just below my hair as I walk her backward until her calves hit the mattress. I stop kissing her long enough to get my shirt up and over my head, then toss it to the floor with the one she just wore.

Her warm palms find my bare chest. The familiar touch sends an inferno coursing through my veins. This is Avery, the woman who knows me better than anyone in the world but who can never know the truth of why I left, why I did what I did to her.

She slowly trails her fingers down over my chest and abdomen, stopping briefly at each one of the scars she's intimately acquainted with, brushing her fingers reverently over them before she finally reaches for the waistband of my jeans. Capturing her lips again, I tangle my tongue with hers while she frees my hard cock and takes it into her small hand.

I groan into her mouth at the pleasure surging through my body, and when she glides her thumb across the head, spreading the pre-cum already seeping out, I have to grit my teeth to keep from coming all over her stomach and fingers.

This is what I've dreamt about. The kiss and touch of the woman who haunts me and curses me. The one I never thought I could live without yet have somehow managed to keep breathing away from over the last four years.

There's one other thing I've lived without, something my mouth waters for and my cock yearns for.

I drop to my knees in front of her and drag her right leg over my shoulder so I can dip my head and glide my tongue through her sweet cunt. She gasps and arches into me, her entire body bending back, head dropping. I wrap my arm around her hips, holding her steady, and she claws at me, her nails scoring my forearms as I continue to devour her and take in the only meal that ever satiated me.

This is dangerous, far more dangerous than even the men after her. To let myself experience this again. To let myself touch her and taste her and feel her hips rolling against my face. To hear her tiny little gasps of pleasure every time my tongue flicks across her clit.

All of it is catastrophically dangerous to both of us.

Still, my fingers itch to feel her, and I glide a hand up her inner thigh and slip two fingers into her heat while my tongue laves at her clit. She moans and squeezes around me, burying her hands in my hair as her legs begin to shake. I tighten my grip on her thighs, holding her steady as I eat her like a starved man.

Because that's what I am—starved for her. For four fucking years...starved of this.

"Oh, God, Kalen..."

Her pussy starts to ripple around my fingers, and I suck her clit between my lips and pulse it in time with curling into that spot inside her that always drove her fucking mad.

She comes, throwing back her head, her mouth falling open. Her entire body spasms, twisting in my arm, her warm sheath clenching and grasping for what it really wants.

I draw out her orgasm as long as I dare until she's gasping and pushing on my head to get me away from her overly sensitive clit. She gazes down at me with glazed-over green eyes that burn with a raging conflagration of need and questions we both know she won't voice right now. I stare up at her, licking her release off my lips, and slowly withdraw my fingers from inside her.

It should end here. Like this. It doesn't matter that my cock aches and screams to get into her wet heat.

I've given her what she needed—a release of her tension, her pain.

That should be it.

I should walk away.

If I were a stronger man, I might, but any strength I had vanished the moment she signed those divorce papers, the moment *this* ended. Instead of leaving like we both know I should, I slowly lower her leg off my shoulder and push to my feet, still gripping her hips.

She watches me in a way that tells me she knows exactly what I'm thinking. For the longest time, she always did. She always knew—what I needed, what I wanted, how to make everything better. That's all I want to do for her now. It's the only thing I can offer.

I brush my lips over hers gently twice, then press my forehead to hers. Her heavy breaths draw me even closer to her quivering body.

Leave now.

Before this goes any further.

Somehow, I find a way to speak. "I should go."

She pulls her head back and runs her hand down to grasp my rigid cock. Her fingers squeeze around it, then she slowly drags her hands along the length, telling me without words that she needs me to stay.

Fuck.

Avery steps backward toward the mattress and sinks down, dragging me with her. I catch myself on my elbow, my body spread out across hers. The warm, familiar feel of her under me has more pre-cum seeping from the head of my cock.

She uses her feet to push my jeans down my thighs to my knees, allowing me to kick them off. Then she reaches between us, spreads her legs, and aligns me with her slick opening.

"Please, Kalen..."

The breathy way she begs for it and says my name makes me push aside all the reasons I shouldn't be doing this and plunge into her. Her pussy contracts around me, welcoming me into the place that's always felt like home. She drops her head back again and gasps, clinging to me, her nails scoring along my shoulders.

"God, Kalen..."

Her words reignite the fire in me, the one that's always blazed for her no matter how hard I've tried to extinguish it over the years—for the good of both of us.

She wraps her legs around my hips, pressing her heels against my lower back to urge me a fraction of an inch deeper. I clench my jaw against the burning coil of release threatening at the base of my spine already. It's been far too fucking long, and this woman means far too much for me to control this. She tightens around my cock—another desperate plea to get me to move, and I take her face between my palms and force her to look at me.

"If you keep doing that, this isn't going to last very long."

Avery swallows thickly and turns her head to tug my ear lobe between her teeth. "Then, we'll just have to do it again."

Jesus fuck.

She is *trying to kill me.*

This woman is trying to pay me back for what I did to her all those years ago, for how I blew up everything and walked away. It's the only explanation for why she would look at me like this, touch me like this, *need* me like this.

But I don't even fucking care.

I issue a low groan, drag back my hips, and plunge

into her again, driving her body down into the shitty, cheap mattress. She groans and gouges my back, rolling her hips to meet each one of my thrusts that I try to keep slow and steady.

If I go any harder, I'll come on the spot, and she needs more than that. She *deserves* more than that.

She's always deserved more than I could give her.

More than I *ever* could.

AVERY

KALEN HAS ALWAYS GIVEN me everything I've ever wanted or at least tried to, and he continues to as he drives into me, grinding his hips and adding a sharp upward thrust at the end that he knows will always catch me in exactly the right spot.

The fact that he has remembered after all these years shouldn't make tears well in my eyes, yet they do. I always knew I could never forget, but I always imagined that when he walked away, he did everything in his power to replace his memories with me with other ones, tried to forget everything we ever were or ever had in any way he could.

I could never do that. Could never let another man touch me. Could never bring myself to even consider it. Maybe because I've been waiting for this moment, for him to come back to me, for us to find a way to get back to *this*.

This is the way it's supposed to be.

Us...

Together...

Our bodies moving in unison.

Completing each other.

Filling all the places that have felt so empty for so long.

Kalen lowers his head and presses his lips to mine. A familiar kiss, the one I've longed to feel again, just like I've craved everything this man does to me when we're in the same room.

The heat that spreads through my body from a single look.

The way his hands know exactly where to touch me, *how* to touch me, to make the entire world disappear.

The way his cock fills me perfectly, making me feel whole for the first time in four years.

I know what asking him for this means, what it might do to him and me, but it's all I want, the only thing that will satiate my hunger and calm the turmoil boiling inside me.

He maintains slow, languid strokes, despite how pent up he appears to be, wound tight like a fucking spring about to snap. His tension builds with my own, and he eases in and out of me, ensuring maximum contact against all the places he knows I need it to send me over the edge again for another mind-numbing orgasm.

The years apart haven't changed how well he

knows me. Kalen was my best friend, the only person I could rely on unquestionably, and he *still* knows me better than anyone.

He knew I would head up to the cabin, even though I haven't been able to go since we split because of the memories it held of the good times we had there. They overshadowed those I had with Gramps, made it too painful to go to the place that once held so much peace. But it was the first place I thought to go because deep down, I knew he would find me there. I *knew* he would understand I needed somewhere safe.

And he found me.

His strong arms have held me so much over the years, and they're doing it now—protecting me and making me forget all the reasons I should be afraid.

In this moment, all the fear is gone. All that exists is this feeling—his touch and his kiss.

He *knows* me and what I need right now.

Just like I know him and what he needs...

I catch his mouth with mine and pull his bottom lip between my teeth, biting down sharply.

His hips jerk wildly. "Fuck!" His entire body tenses even more, and I suck on his lip to ease the sharp sting before releasing it with a pop. "Fucking hell, Avery."

A strong hand tightens at my hip as the other cradles my face. I roll my hips up to meet his, spurring him to increase the pace, to get us both to what we're chasing—freedom. From our past. From the unsettled future. From all the dangers and uncertainty.

Those little bites of pain, the slight aggression, the

scratches and the screams, it always pushed him over the edge. Always drove him mad. Always made him become what I knew he wanted to be when we were locked together physically like this, especially at the end. By then, I wasn't having sex with Kalen; I was having sex with Chaos. But this...this is some strange mixture of the two. Like he can't decide which one he's supposed to be in this moment.

Maybe he doesn't know.

God knows I don't.

The two are so entwined that they can't be separated anymore.

This is all I'll ever get of Kalen. All that's left is tainted and twisted by what Chaos has done. But he's still beautiful, still the strong, reliable, loving man I've always loved, deep down at his core. I know that; I'm just not sure he does anymore.

I squeeze around him, tightening with each retreat of his hips to keep the head of his cock dragging along that perfect spot, and his pace increases, every thrust building another orgasm deep inside me, in that place only *he* could ever reach.

Tears trickle down my cheeks—of pain, of hope, of regret.

There's so much he doesn't know, so much he never gave me the chance to explain, so much we could have been if he hadn't shut me out and given me no choice. The truth would destroy him, though, exactly as it has me since that day four years ago when I put ink on those papers that officially ended it all. So as much as I want to come clean, want to tell him everything, I'll keep it bottled up inside me the same way he does all his pain.

The pain that propels him on now, even when this feels so incredible. I can see it in the way he looks at me, the darkness in his eyes that never used to be there. Whatever it was that drove him away from me back then is driving him to do this now, to try to fix what's been broken in me by this entire situation.

And it's working.

Pleasure ripples across my heated skin and floods my veins. My body winds impossibly tighter, part of me not wanting to let go because it will mean an end to *this* moment with Kalen. I don't want to lose it, don't want to lose *him* again. I fight it with everything I have until my limbs are shaking violently and my chest is heaving with my effort. He presses his mouth to mine and twists our tongues, more frantic than the earlier kisses.

He's losing his restraint, his ability to control Chaos. There was a time not that long ago when that might have scared me, when I might have wondered where he was in his head if not here with me, but I know he's with me now. His blue eyes meet mine, holding the same heat and passion I've always felt from him, the same love, the same turmoil remain, just like the last few times we were together before our lives imploded.

His jaw clenches so hard that it almost looks painful, and he reaches between us to find my clit. He's close to coming and needs me to come first. I'm right there, and this man understands me well enough to know it.

He rolls his thumb over my most sensitive spot, and lights flicker in my vision, the orgasm just on the edge of the horizon. His lips crash against mine, catching my gasps and moans, and I kiss him like it's our last time, like I would have if I had known back then.

The heat building in my abdomen becomes almost unbearable with my effort to prolong this, but he adjusts his position and drives even harder, feeling the difference in my body, knowing what I need. He pinches my clit and rolls his hips, grinding his pelvis into his hand, adding more friction as the head of his cock drags against my G-spot until I finally blow.

My pussy clenches around him tightly, and he buries his face against my neck and issues a deep groan, emptying himself inside me. My hips buck wildly, seeking more even as the pleasure threatens to drown me.

Waves of ecstasy crash over me, relentlessly stealing my breath, while all the pain floats away on a cloud made of this perfect moment in time. It drags on for what feels like forever, my body reveling in the release of everything that's been weighing me down, fragmenting the worries and agonies of the past and letting them go.

Kalen's heart hammers against mine, its rhythm an old song my heart knows well, as his body continues to move with mine.

Finally, as my orgasm starts to wane, he freezes and then sags against me, rolling slightly to one side to keep his weight off me, his cock still hard and buried inside where I need him most.

His hurried, warm breaths flutter against my cheek, and he sweeps his lips over my heated skin softly, barely there, featherlight and holding so many unspoken truths. This might be it, our final time together, our last chance to hold one another and experience what it's like to be with someone who completes you fully.

Tomorrow is uncertain.

Nothing is guaranteed, especially not with the nightmare we face.

But we have tonight.

We have *now*.

I let my eyes drift closed. His strong arm wrapped around my chest holds the incredibly blissful feeling overtaking me in place, keeps me from falling away, back to the dark place I was in when I woke. He grounds me in a way nothing else ever could.

Having Kalen at my side and watching my back is the only way I'll ever survive this. He holds my life and my heart in his capable hands that lightly brush over my skin as we lie here together.

The feel of his body pressed to mine and the post-orgasmic exhaustion finally start to drag me under with a sense of calm and rightness I didn't know I could find again.

Too bad it won't be there when I wake up.

10

CHAOS

I release a frustrated sigh, pinching the bridge of my nose. "Tell me you got something, Preacher..."

Reaper, Mouth, Viktoria, and I all stare at my phone on the counter, waiting with bated breath for Preacher to start talking.

"Oh, I have plenty." He offers a light chuckle. "I just don't know you're going to want to hear it."

Fucking hell.

"Shit." I scrub my hand over my face. That wasn't exactly what I hoped to hear from the man when he finally called with information on Perez. "That bad?"

The sound of his fingers flying over the keyboard floats through the line. "That bad."

Reaper releases an annoyed sigh. "*Well*, get on with it!"

None of us have any patience this morning, not after what we saw and did at *South of the Border* last night.

Preacher offers a huff at Reaper's tone. "Using the information Avery gave us the other night, I've been able to do a deep dive into this guy, and none of it is good."

Shit.

"I don't know how this fucker has stayed under the radar of the DEA and FBI because he is one bad moth-erfucker, or is at least *tied* to some. I traced the holding company listed as the owner of all of his businesses back to another holding company, and another, and another, and after about fifteen layers or shit, eventu-ally to a trucking company in Merida, Mexico."

"Fuck." My eyes meet Reaper's. "Cartel?"

Preacher issues a humorless laugh. "It certainly looks that way. In that area, the number and type of trucks, the money being spent...this guy is either traf-ficking and selling it, or he is laundering the money. Likely both."

I nod even though he can't see me and exchange a knowing look with Reaper and Mouth. "That's exactly what I thought last night after what we found."

More clicking sounds come through the line as Preacher pulls up whatever he's looking for. "I checked DEA and FBI databases. This guy isn't even anywhere on their radar. So, he must be pretty good at what he does, or at least he's good at hiding it."

"Yeah, the restaurant seemed like a decent front,

but after last night, he's gonna have some eyes on him." I lean back against the wall and cross my arms over my chest. "That amount of cash, if any of it survived that fire, the cops are going to want to know what the fuck was going on in that back room."

"I'm assuming that was intentional to draw his focus away from Avery?"

"Definitely, but I don't know if it did any good or not. I just wanted that fucker to suffer for what he has already done to her."

What I might have made worse last night.

It made sense at the time. Seemed like the right thing in that heat of the moment, when she was so terrified, so desperate to feel safe, but as soon as the fuzzy haze of my orgasm fully dissolved, I knew what I had done, how badly I'd complicated things by giving in to her.

Preacher's low chuckle crackles through the line. "Well, if you really want to make this guy pay, I've been able to locate a few more businesses in the area that Avery wasn't aware of that could potentially be drop houses and warehouses for storage of cash or drugs. I'll text you the updated list."

I nod slowly. "Good..."

The more places we can hit him, the more he will hurt until I can finally get my hands on the man himself.

Reaper raises an eyebrow at me. "What's our next play, Chaos? What do you want to do?"

This typically would be all Reaper's call. He's the

one who put this crew together, technically the leader of our ragtag group. The one who always calls the shots on our missions, but he's looking to me because Avery is *my* responsibility.

Thank fuck, none of them know what happened last night.

If anyone suspected I ended up in bed with her, it would make things a whole lot more complicated than it already is, and I'd never hear the fucking end of it. Especially from Viktoria—who already eyes me like she suspects something even though I've given her no reason to.

I was out here within five minutes of Avery falling asleep, so there's no way anyone can know what went down in that bedroom. But I can't think about it. This is precisely why it was such a horrible idea because I need to be concentrating on our plan of attack, not how good her cunt felt wrapped around my cock or how her kiss made me feel alive again for the first time in years.

Tapping my foot against the wall, I consider our options. We don't know enough about Perez's connection to the cartel or his current operations. That makes unease tighten my gut. "Taking out this guy locally won't be an issue. Reaper, Mouth, and I can handle it easily. But if he is someone the cartel relies on, if he's a big player in their organization, hell, even a medium-sized one, they're not going to look too kindly upon us destroying their network here."

Preacher types some more. "He has places in Baltimore, DC, and almost every city between there and Philly. He's likely controlling an entire region."

Reaper scowls. "Fuck, that definitely isn't good."

Mouth nods in agreement from where he stands near the door, hip propped against the wall, brow furrowed, and lips pressed in a hard line.

"No." I shake my head. "It's not. Going after the cartel would be a suicide mission, so we concentrate on this guy. If his accountant was onto him and he had to take her out, then he fucked up bad enough to let Avery see what they had done, he's not going to want to let his higher-ups in the cartel know that. If he reveals his own fuck-up, that puts his neck out there."

Vik finally speaks up, shifting where she sits on the counter. "So you think if we eliminate him, we remove any threat against her?"

Acid churns in my stomach at the thought that I could be wrong. "I sure as fuck hope so. I think it's our only play right now."

Reaper glances at me. "But where do we start?"

The sound of Preacher's fingers flying across the keyboard come through the line again. "He has a warehouse not far from the restaurant you toasted last night. From what I was able to get from hacking into some cameras at some surrounding businesses, he's there almost daily. But he keeps it locked up pretty tight. About a dozen men at any given time."

Reaper grins. "It's never stopped us before."

I chuckle and shake my head at the clear reference to what we did in New York to the Russian human trafficking ring. The Yankovich assholes never saw us coming and didn't stand a chance against Vik and the three of us. Still, Vik and Reaper both ended up with holes in them.

This time, let's hope everybody stays out of the path of gunfire.

Tilting my head side to side, I try to release the tension suddenly building at the top of my spine. "If we're truly going to take out this guy, we can't just hit one or two places. We need to eliminate his entire operation—every single one—and we need to do it fast so he doesn't have time to figure out what's happening and set up better protection."

Reaper nods his agreement. "Preach, how many businesses total that you can find within a hundred miles of here?"

"Thirteen."

"Fuck..." I rub at my neck, a throbbing starting to work up into my head. "That's a lot for the three of us to hit—"

"Four of us!" Viktoria's annoyed comment comes sharp and direct, pointed squarely at me.

"*Three.* You need to stay here with Avery."

Vik scowls. "You said it yourself—no one's going to find her here."

A low growl starts in my throat. "I'm not going to leave her alone."

She huffs an annoyed sigh and continues to glare at me. With her skill-set, she doesn't like to be sidelined from the action, but keeping Avery safe is the entire point of all this. Leaving her alone, even somewhere I know can't be traced back to her, isn't going to happen.

Reaper gives his woman a pointed look before returning his attention to me. "What happens if we take out all these places and attract the attention of the cartel? What if it turns out he is important enough for them to come looking for whoever took him out?"

It's the last thing we want, but we can't ignore the possibility.

"We deal with it when that time comes."

Preacher clears his throat, reminding us he's still on the line. "You really want to fight an entire cartel?"

That's a fair question, but it still raises my hackles coming from Preacher. He, of all people, should know the lengths any of us would go to in order to protect the people we care about.

"If it means Avery will be safe, I'll go to Mexico myself, find the head of the snake, and fucking bite it off."

AVERY

"You're going to Mexico?" My question comes out soft, barely a whisper, more like it's said to myself than meant for the room, but all eyes turn toward me where I stand just outside the bedroom door.

Kalen's gaze locks with mine, and his shoulders

tense and jaw tightens. He shifts against the wall and shakes his head. "No. Just talking."

"Is that Avery?" A voice comes from a phone set on the counter.

I glance at it with a raised brow. "Um...yeah?"

"Hey, Avery. I'm doing everything I can to help you stay clear of this fucker."

Kalen inclines his head toward the phone. "Preacher."

"Oh, thanks, Preacher."

Despite how long he's been friends with the guys, I never got to meet the man in person. I could never have imagined I'd one day be needing his kind of help. Then again, there are a lot of things I never thought would happen.

I never thought Kalen and I would grow so far apart that we could never find our way back to each other. I never thought I'd see someone so close to me killed in such a brutal way. I never thought I would end up back in Kalen's arms the way I did last night after everything that happened between us. And for some reason, despite all the evidence pointing to exactly what would happen, I never expected to wake up alone this morning.

You're a fucking idiot, Avery.

He never slept in the same bed a single night with me after he came home from the hospital. We would fuck and kiss and be frantic for each other, but as soon as it was done, he would slip out of the bed we once shared and sleep on the recliner alone.

Why did I think last night would be any different?

Just because I needed him. Just because I wanted him in that moment of weakness. That doesn't *change* anything.

He gave me all he could and then left, and now, he's standing here, acting like nothing even happened, looking at me with the same wall between us as he's had for the last four years.

Last night was a single desperate act between two people seeking something—me comfort, him a release. Maybe he was right when he said he shouldn't stay, when he tried to walk out before anything happened. It might have been smarter to ignore the desire, the pulsating, living, breathing attraction that always seemed to exist between us. But now it's too late to go back.

If it was a mistake, we've made it and have to deal with the fallout. Which for Kalen apparently means pretending it didn't happen.

I tear my gaze from his and scan the room, taking in the concerned looks of everyone else. From what little I heard when I made it to the door, the level of danger we're all facing has skyrocketed with the information Preacher sent. "So...what are you guys going to do?"

The boys exchange a look, and Viktoria smiles at me.

She offers a slight shrug. "We have a plan. Sort of. I'll stay here as your babysitter, and the boys go do what they do best."

I lock eyes with Kalen again, unease creeping up my spine, a cold sweat breaking out across my skin. "Are-are you going to kill him?"

They all exchange glances again, and Viktoria finally offers me a sympathetic look, but the guys certainly don't. I wouldn't expect them to. When it comes right down to it, these men are all highly skilled killers, and just because they're "retired" doesn't mean they've stopped. The security company they've formed does a hell of a lot more than serve rich and powerful men and women who need protection from violent lovers. They're mercenaries for hire, and I didn't even have to pay them to want to kill Ricardo.

The thought of more blood being spilled makes bile climb my throat.

Kalen steps off the wall, his hands fisting at his sides. "This dude is bad news, Avery. Last night, at *South of the Border*, we found millions of dollars in cash stacked in a back room, and Preacher has linked him and his business to one of the cartels in Merida."

"What?"

Millions of dollars?

A cartel?

I shake my head. "No. No. That's not possible. He's so nice..."

Kalen's jaw hardens again. "Remember what he did to your friend, Avery. What he would have done to do you, too."

I flinch at the comment and regret instantly flashes in Kalen's blue eyes.

"I'm sorry, that was harsh." He lets out a frustrated sigh and shakes his head. "You just have to understand that men like this put on a good façade. They know how to make people around them feel comfortable and safe. Their goal is to ensure no one ever suspects they could possibly be involved in anything like this. That's the entire point. The cartel uses people who will never be suspected." He watches me for my reaction, but his words are only slowly sinking in. "This guy is in *deep*, Avery. And with the kind of people he's tied up with, he isn't going to stop coming for you until he's physically prevented from doing it anymore."

Any icy shiver rolls through my spine. I wrap my arms around myself and rub at the goosebumps on my bare skin. Visions of Amelia's dead, staring eyes flash through my mind again.

"I'm sorry. I just—"

I can't seem to get out the words, can't seem to swallow whatever is choking me. Four hard sets of eyes watch me, trying to figure out what's going on. I stumble backward toward the bedroom, close the door, and throw the lock before the tears start to flow again.

They're killing people. They have to. More than just Ricardo. They're going to kill anyone who gets in their way.

And it's all my fault...

A sharp knock at the door jerks me away from it, and I swipe at the tears on my cheeks.

"Avery..." Kalen's deep voice rumbles through the piece of wood separating us. The knob turns, and he tries to push it open. It doesn't budge, and he mutters something under his breath that makes my chest tighten. "Avery, unlock the fucking door, or I'll break it down."

He will.

That's not a threat.

It's a promise.

I unlock the door with a shaking hand, and the second it clicks, he shoves it open and stalks in, slamming it closed behind him.

Anger flashes in his gaze, and for the first time I can remember in all the years I've known him, it's actually directed at me. "Don't ever lock that fucking door again. What if I needed to get to you quickly?" His eyes widen as he takes me in, and his expression softens, his shoulders releasing a bit of the tension there. "Why did you run away? Why are you crying?"

"I-I..."

How do I explain this to a man who has no qualms about killing someone if he believes there's a reason?

"You're going to kill him, Kalen. You're going to kill Ricardo and anyone else who gets in the way."

He takes a step toward me, his lips curling into a sneer. "Damn fucking right I am. The man is trying to *kill* you, Avery, and he won't stop until he succeeds or until something stops him. That something is *me*."

"I know." I swallow back the emotion clogging my throat. "And I know I came to you for help, but he has a wife...kids. Couldn't you talk to him?"

"*Talk* to him?" Kalen throws up his hands. "Jesus,

Avery, I know you're not this naïve. You don't really believe that would work."

"No..." I shake my head. "You're right. I'm not—"

"We aren't touching his wife and kids. They more than likely have no idea what's going on or how he's making his money, but Avery, listen to me." He steps forward and captures my face in his palms. "He and his organization cannot continue like this. If they do, not only are you in danger but so is anyone else who gets in their way. The only way I can protect you is—"

"To be Chaos," I finish the sentence for him, and his eyes harden again.

"Yes."

"Is that why you left last night?"

"Shit." He drops his hand from my face and scrubs it over his own. When his eyes meet mine again, a recognizable pain lives deep in them. "Last night was a mistake, Avery. I can't...we can't make it again." He takes a step back and reaches for the door. "My focus needs to be on protecting you and ending this threat. I can't be worried about your safety when you're in the one place you shouldn't have to."

He yanks open the door, steps out, and slams it closed behind him.

Worry about my safety in the one place I shouldn't have to?

His words ring in my ears.

What the hell is he talking about?

11

CHAOS

Sometimes, the things that seem the most innocuous can hold the worst danger, pose the greatest threat. The cinderblock warehouse in the rundown industrial area should be housing produce and restaurant supplies—as it advertises on the outside—but I know what's really hidden behind its walls.

A madman lurks inside, intent on destroying Avery for no other reason but that she stumbled upon something she shouldn't have and could get in his way.

According to what Preacher sent us this morning, this is his primary place of operation. The warehouse and offices where Avery worked were the face of the business only. This is where the real shit goes down.

Vehicles come and go constantly, at least two or three an hour. Even if Perez's business is flourishing, there is no way there would be this kind of heavy traffic with just deliveries for the restaurants. The trucks with Mexican plates tie directly to and confirm the information Preacher got us, and watching frantic men pulling up in expensive rides and rushing in proves what we did last night sent them into disarray.

Which means my plan worked.

Perez won't be concentrating on his search for Avery when he is trying to figure out who blew up his fucking restaurant and burned his millions.

We're in the right place to take out this fucker.

This guy has been getting away with it for far too long, manipulating people like Avery, who believe in the genuine goodness of people and are trusting and loyal. She had no idea who she was working for, and it's gotten her stuck in this quagmire.

But hopefully, it will end tonight.

Perez's car has been parked out front since before we even got here. He likely came here right after the explosion at *South of the Border* to do some damage control and to try to protect whatever it is he keeps in this warehouse.

The plans Preacher got for us showed four loading docks and multiple entrances, which makes it more difficult for Reaper, Mouth, and me to cover alone. But we don't have much of a choice. We can't wait for backup after what we did last night.

Perez might not know who was behind it, likely suspects it's a rival here in town, but our anonymity can only last so long. In a world with so many cameras, if we happen to get caught on one and he manages to ID us, Avery will be the one who pays the price for our actions.

I'll never allow that to happen.

I glance at Reaper and Mouth. "You guys ready?"

They both nod.

With Mouth's rifle aimed at the warehouse, no one is getting out of here alive.

"If you see that fucker come out, you put a fucking bullet through his heart."

The corners of Mouth's lips curl up. This is what he lives for, and knowing he's able to contribute to our very worthy mission will do wonders for him.

My count is still at ten inside the warehouse, but that doesn't mean more aren't there who haven't shown themselves yet. I would say this should be a simple in and out, but nothing is ever that easy, and thinking it will be is what gets people killed...or worse.

No one is getting hurt tonight except these cartel assholes who deserve it.

We get in. Take out everyone. Gather as much information as we can to help us shut down the rest of the operation. Make sure no one else is coming for Avery.

It's a simple plan. One we've executed a hundred times together over our years in service. It's one we could do in our sleep. But we won't be sleeping tonight. We'll be wiping out a part of what keeps Perez's business running, including anyone who tries to flee. It's hard to escape Mouth's shot, and he's raring to go.

Equipped with our night vision goggles, Reaper and I take off in the direction of the loading docks. If this place is what we think it is, the security here will be a lot better than at the restaurant. But the fucker wasn't smart enough to hook up this facility to a generator.

I check my watch.

11:53...

Two more minutes until show time.

Reaper and I wait until exactly 11:55, and the entire twenty-block radius goes dark.

Right on time, Preach.

That man can hack anything, and the dark brought by his shutting down this area of the grid gives us the advantage even on their home turf. Perez's men will be scrambling.

Reaper and I don't waste any time making our move to the rear door near the docks. I set a charge on the handle, we step back, and I blow it instantly. The small blast does the job, the door easily swinging open, granting us access.

Confused shouts in Spanish fill the air, and men scurry away from the blast down the hall, illuminated only by a single-bulb emergency lamp. Reaper quickly shoots the two men and then the light, plunging us into complete darkness.

These fuckers thought they could go after an innocent woman who had no way to protect herself. They have no idea what they've just brought down upon themselves.

A tidal wave of pain is about to engulf them.

I reach into the bag slung over my shoulder, grab the first charge, and set it at one of the main load-bearing walls. According to the blueprints, I can bring down this entire place easily.

We hustle down the hallway toward the next target location. Voices approach, and Reaper takes the three men out with quick shots. Perez may have armed his employees, but they're wholly unprepared for someone coming in guns blazing.

Continued shouts and talking alert us to precisely where they are the deeper we get into the complex. We easily put them down—one by one.

The hallway intersects with another, and we pause and listen for the sound of anyone approaching, but all that greets us is an eerie quiet.

I signal to Reaper. He nods, and we go on three, turning the corner and instantly meeting gunfire. Bullets slam into the wall to my left, but our return fusillade of shots takes them down and allows us to pass to the next location for a charge.

With the second one set in place, we continue through the maze of hallways, clearing each room as we go.

Two down. Two to go.

Once I'm done, all that will be left of this place is a pile of smoking rubble and ash, but it isn't my primary mission tonight. Finding the fucker, Perez, is.

Where the hell is he?

We move deeper into the warehouse complex, but

there isn't any sign of the man after Avery, only his minions, who we easily pick off.

The radio in my ear crackles with three taps, the signal from Mouth that he took out three men who either tried to flee or were coming in to assist. He would have given us a different signal if he thought any of them were Perez, which means we still need to find the asshole—and fast.

Though this area's mostly industrial, that doesn't mean there isn't somebody inside one of the nearby buildings this time of night who might hear the gunfire and alert the authorities. The last thing we need is to get caught here like this. Then not only would Avery be a sitting duck, but we'd likely go to prison for the rest of our lives.

Using the skills Uncle Sam gives you to become a mercenary vigilante is frowned upon in certain circles, mainly the ones frequented by people who put you in cuffs.

We need to get Perez and get out quickly, and now, we've finally reached the main massive warehouse area. It's the only place we haven't searched yet.

I pause for a moment to take stock. Mouth took out three outside, and we've hit four in here. That means probably three more, plus Perez, are somewhere in the building.

The warehouse itself is vast, with any number of hiding spots. This is where things get dicey, and I'd kill to have a full team here. Having Cutter and Flash with us would have made me feel a lot better about this, but there wasn't any time to wait for them to get to town. The immediate threat calls for immediate action.

Something rustles in the corner behind a large stack of pallets, and I signal Reaper. We approach cautiously, so quietly, there's no way whoever's back there will know we're coming.

We turn the corner and unleash into the two men with their backs propped up against a pallet. Their weapons tumble to the ground before they have a chance to fire, and I step over them and pump a few more rounds into each one to ensure they're not getting back up.

Reaper continues to scan the warehouse for any signs of movement, but it's far too quiet. If anyone else is still in here, they're laying low, doing their best to conceal themselves from us until they think the coast is clear.

They underestimate our ability to sniff out a rat.

Row by row.

Pallet after pallet.

Box after box.

We make our way through the warehouse, checking every nook and cranny possible.

There's nowhere to hide from us when we're on a mission.

A man tries to rush at us from between two massive crates, but his reaction time is so slow. Reaper ends him before he can pull the trigger.

"Where the fuck is Perez?"

Reaper inclines his head toward a small office off to

one side of the warehouse, and I place the final two charges along the far wall as we make our way toward it, one of us always watching our backs.

But as soon as we step in, it's clear Perez isn't here anymore.

Open desk drawers.

Empty file cabinets.

Folders and papers strewn across the floor.

It definitely looks like this was Perez's office while he was doing business here, but whatever was in here is long gone.

Reaper and I sift through some of the discarded items on the floor. "He must have come in his car and left in the back of one of the trucks where we couldn't see him."

"Fuck!"

We missed him.

He holds up a paper to me. I tear it out of his hand and scan it in the moonlight coming in from a single window. The same address Preacher gave us for the company in Mexico draws my eye.

"You think he went there?"

Reaper offers a half-shrug. "It's possible. He may be going to smooth things over after his losses last night, or he may have gone to hide out."

"Shit."

I storm out of the office and back into the warehouse, over to one of the pallets, pulling out my knife. It easily slices through the plastic wrapped around the boxes, and I pull out one and hold it up.

"Boxes of dried fruit?"

No fucking way.

Reaper takes it from me and tears it open, pouring the contents onto the concrete floor. Dried apple chips come first, followed by tightly packaged stacks of cash. "Well, damn."

He drops the box and approaches a different stack. I join him and cut it open, grabbing one of the boxes and tearing into it.

"I think we have the answer about what they're doing." I hold up a large brick wrapped in duct tape.

Reaper grabs it and cuts it open, bringing up white powder on his knife.

"Cocaine?"

"Sure looks like it."

"So, he's dealing and laundering money. How the fuck did Avery get herself into this?"

"I don't know, man, but it seems Perez went south of the border—pun intended. You know what that means..."

I shove my knife back into my boot and follow him toward the door. "I sure as hell do."

The only way to end this is to go after him.

We'll check his house and all the other locations Preacher gave us before we head back to my place, but if we don't find him, then we're going south, too.

AVERY

THE CHINESE TAKEOUT Viktoria basically forced me to eat earlier sits like a lead weight in my stomach, heavier the longer the guys are gone. Any attempt at sleep would be useless—my mind and body far too restless to relax.

Between what happened last night with Kalen, the information Preacher provided this morning, and what I know the guys are doing right now, I'm back to being as big of a mess as I was when I fell into bed with Kalen.

With nothing else to do inside the apartment besides sit and wait, I pace along the already-worn ancient wood floors.

Back and forth.

Back and forth.

Back and forth between the recliner and the TV that plays some stupid rom-com movie I am in no mood to watch.

Viktoria glances up from her phone from her usual spot sitting on top of the counter. "Please stop that. You're making me nervous."

Shoving my hands back through my hair, I shake my head. "I'm sorry. I can't help it." I glance at the clock on the microwave for what feels like the millionth time. Only eight minutes have passed since I last checked it. "They've been gone a long time."

"They'll be gone a while. They're heading to what Preacher thinks is the primary location for Perez's operations here. They have to do recon before they can go in, and they might face some resistance."

Resistance.

"You mean get shot."

"Don't be a pessimist." Vik releases a heavy sigh and slides off the counter to walk over to the fridge and pull it open. Holding up a bottle of red wine, she jiggles it from side to side. "You need some of this."

"Where did that come from?"

It's certainly not something Kalen would willingly keep stocked.

A grin plays on her lips. "I thought you might need a little something to calm you down, so I brought it with me. You were too busy obsessing over your ex-husband, so you didn't even notice it when I got here."

I wince at her easy observation, then do my best to brush it off. "I was not obsessing."

Vik barks out a laugh as she twists the top off the bottle. "Honey, you should have seen the look on your face when he walked out that door." She shakes her head and makes a little *tsking* sound as she opens a cabinet and pulls out two glasses. "The tension between you two. Seriously." She fans herself, then fills a glass for each of us and pushes one toward me. "Drink that."

I scowl at her but take a sip anyway. Alcohol is likely not the best way to deal with the current stressful situation, but I'm not about to turn it down right now. With my nerves this frayed and no sign of the guys coming back anytime soon, anything that might help relieve a little of the tension is welcome.

The sharp tannins hit my tongue, and I almost

release a little sigh at the sweet, fruity flavor. Even though it's far too soon to be feeling any of the effects of the alcohol in my system, some of the pain in my shoulders releases.

Vik watches me over the top of her glass. "You slept with him, didn't you?"

I jerk my head up, my body immediately tightening and going stock straight. "What?"

A grin tilts Viktoria's lips. "I *said*, you slept with him, *didn't* you? Last night..."

Fucking hell...

I stare into my drink and contemplate denying it for a moment, but Viktoria was a decorated NYPD detective before she left the force to be with Reaper, and she's not going to let me get away with it. She'll interrogate me until I break, wear me down until I can't hold it in any longer, and I don't have the energy to fight her.

"Yes."

She slaps her hand on the counter, making me jump. "I knew it. I fucking *knew* it." Her grins spreads wider, eyes alight with humor and interest. "The minute I walked in here and saw Chaos' face, I knew it."

"Please don't make a big deal about this."

She gapes at me. "Don't make a big deal about this? After the conversation we had the other night...really?"

I sigh and pinch the bridge of my nose against the threatening headache. Another drink of my wine gives me an excuse to consider my response and offers a bit of liquid courage to open this avenue of discussion. "It doesn't mean anything. He said it was a mistake."

She snorts and takes a sip of her wine. "Of course he did."

Ouch.

"What's that supposed to mean?"

"God love ya, Avery. For such a smart woman, you sure are blind when it comes to that man. Whatever happened between you two, it isn't over, and"—she holds up a hand to stop me from interrupting—"don't say it's just sex. Don't say he was just comforting you because you were upset."

I press my lips together to stop myself from interjecting and saying just that because that's what it *was*. Kalen made that very clear to me this morning. It was great while it lasted, but he won't let it happen again.

Viktoria locks her gaze with mine, suddenly serious. "Because it's more than that. You two have unfinished business. Things to say to each other that, for some reason, neither of you are saying, and it's about time you did and stop dancing around each other—for both your sakes."

For both your sakes.

That was why we got divorced, why we ended this in the first place. To save both of us the pain we were causing each other. He couldn't stand to be in the same room with me unless we were having sex, and I couldn't handle knowing he didn't love me anymore.

We were at a painful crossroads and going different ways, and that's the way it would have stayed had I not stumbled upon what Perez was doing. More than likely, we never would have seen each other again, each living with the memories of our mistakes.

I squeeze my eyes closed and shake my head. "It's not that easy. When this is over, we'll just go our separate ways again."

She raises a dark eyebrow. "You really believe that? That both of you are just going to walk away and go back to how things were before this mess with Perez?"

I nod and take a sip of wine.

Viktoria barks out another laugh and shakes her head, a smile curling her lips. "Let me clue you in on a little something I've learned during my many years interrogating suspects—"

"What? I'm a suspect now?"

She grins at me. "I'm going to tell you something I think is obvious, at least to someone like me who watches body language and knows how to find someone's *tell*. I'm sure whatever happened between you and Kalen hurt both of you in ways I can never fathom. I've seen Reaper struggling. So, I can imagine what it was like when they came back from that mission where Kalen and Mouth got hurt. That would have been right around the time you're talking about." She shakes her head. "These are not the type of men who are going to want to openly talk about their feelings or who will admit they've made mistakes, who are going to ask for forgiveness. That's something I knew the moment I met Reaper, and I'm sure you knew it.

"So, if you're waiting for him to tell you he's sorry

and somehow make amends, it will never happen. You need to be the one to bridge the gap. You need to be the one to tell him how you feel."

"What if I don't know how I feel?"

Her green eyes roll, and she smirks. "Then you're lying. You know *exactly* how you feel. You just don't want to admit it to yourself or me."

I tighten my hand around the glass, staring down into the red liquid. Harsh memories assault me from every side, ones I've tried so hard to keep buried. "There are things Kalen doesn't know…"

She raises an eyebrow. "Things like what?"

Things I promised myself I would never voice, never tell anyone. Saying it out loud makes it real, forces me to face the pain and guilt, but at the same time, Viktoria feels like more of a friend than I've had in a long time. And she's spent far more time with Kalen than I have recently. She might be able to provide some insight.

"If I tell you, you have to promise *never* to tell Kalen. If he ever found out, it would destroy him."

She slowly lowers her glass from her lips and sets it on the counter. "This sounds serious."

"It is. So, please, don't say anything. You can't."

I'm not even sure I can say this.

"I promise. I won't."

I inhale slowly, closing my eyes for a moment to try to center myself and keep from crying before I even get out the words that I've kept bottled up for so long.

A car door slams outside, and Viktoria rushes

toward the window and peeks out between the blinds. "It's them." She turns back to me. "You have about thirty seconds before they get up here. So, if you want to get this off your chest, do it quickly."

Thirty seconds to drop this bomb.

But the words are already there, sitting on the tip of my tongue, waiting and ready. I let them rush out as fast as I can before the knob turns and the door pushes open.

Viktoria stares at me, mouth hung open slightly as Kalen, Reaper, and Mouth enter.

Kalen's gaze darts between the two of us, brow furrowed. "What's wrong?"

Everything.

And now, I don't even have time to explain anything to her.

Vik shakes her head and forces a smile. "Nothing. Everything's fine. Avery was just getting worried about you guys." She turns to me. "I told you there was nothing to worry about."

I swallow thickly, trying to prevent the tears from falling. "I know."

It's a lie.

There are so many things to worry about—too many to count.

12

AVERY

As soon as the door closes behind Reaper, Viktoria, and Mouth, Kalen throws the lock and turns to me, arms crossed over his chest. "Tell me what's wrong."

I take a sip of my wine and turn back toward the kitchen so he can't see my face and read me like an open book the way he always has. "I told you...nothing. I was just worried." I offer a little half-smile over my shoulder as I put the cap back on the wine bottle and return it to the fridge. "But you're back now, so—"

"You're lying."

Shit.

I jerk upright at his voice so close to me, my heart hammering in my chest. The damn man moves like a ghost. I hadn't even noticed he came up behind me. Slowly, I turn around to find him only inches from my face. His tall, powerful body dwarfs mine, his anger evident in his stance and the set of his shoulders.

"Do you think I'm stupid, Avery? You think I don't know you well enough to know when you're lying? When you're keeping something from me?" He shakes his head, offering a sardonic grin. "Plus, Viktoria did a shit job hiding her face when we walked in. What were you two talking about? What's wrong?"

I shake my head, looking at the cracked linoleum floor rather than at him. "Please, Kalen. Just drop it. It was nothing."

He uses his calloused hand to lift my chin until my eyes meet his. "Don't lie to me, Avery. I have *never* lied to you."

Bullshit.

I could call him out on *that* lie. I could tell him he lied when he told me he would love me forever. When he told me he would never leave. When he told me I would never be alone again. But that would just start a massive fight we don't need to have right now, not with everything else going on.

It doesn't matter anymore. What does is that he and the guys are safe while trying to keep *me* safe.

They remained suspiciously silent about what happened tonight and the plan going forward when they got back, and Kalen ushered them out before anything was said about it, leaving me in the dark with the confession I had just made to Viktoria.

One I wish I could take back now that it's out in the

world, and one I can't reveal to Kalen. His demand that I come clean will only end in more pain.

"Please tell me what happened tonight, Kalen. Did you find Perez?"

He studies me for a moment, hand still clutching my chin, almost like he's debating whether or not to let his line of questioning go and my aversion slide. "We didn't get Perez. But we will. We're leaving tomorrow. We'll be gone for a few days this time. You don't need to worry about what happens next."

The wine churns in my stomach, suddenly harsh and acidic when it had been so fruity and delicious only moments ago. "A few days?" That can only mean one thing. "Are you going to Mexico?"

His jaw hardens, and he slowly releases my chin, almost reluctantly pulling his hand away. "That's where he went. So, that's where we're going."

"But you *can't*. If he's connected to a cartel, there's no way you can go up against them." I shake my head. "Just no. You can't go!"

He takes a step toward me, and I instinctively back away until my shoulders hit the refrigerator behind me —not because I fear he will hurt me, but because I fear what I will do if I let the man get close to me again.

"I told you I was going to protect you, that I would make this guy pay for what he did. If that means going to Mexico and taking out fifty of his fucking men, I'll do it. I'll do anything to keep you safe."

"But there are only three of you."

"We're calling in some help, babe. I promise—everything's gonna be okay."

Everything's gonna be okay...

He has said those words to me so many times over the years, made that promise, yet I have a hard time believing anything he says. Not when he returned full of holes and acting like a totally different person. Not when he's looking me in the eyes with an intensity that can only be Chaos when what I want to see is Kalen.

"Do you believe me, Avery? Do you trust that I'll fix this?"

"I know you'll try, but if you got hurt or—"

His hand circles my bicep and tightens. "Listen to me...that's not going to happen. We're going to go down there. We're going to remove the threat, and we're going to come the fuck home."

I close my eyes and take a shaky breath to keep from releasing a sob or calling him out on the truth. He and I both know there's a chance he won't come back. There's a chance none of them will, but he needs to hear me say I believe it. He needs the confidence that I'll be okay while he's gone and won't worry myself sick over something I can't control.

He needs me to lie.

I open my eyes and meet his hard sapphire gaze again. "Okay. I believe you'll take care of things, come back, and everything will be fine."

"Exactly."

We stand, staring at each other for what feels like forever. Familiar tension twists at my core the longer he keeps his blue eyes on me. They gleam with a hunger for something, but not for anything in the goddamn fridge behind me.

He might not return, and we both need what one more night together can give us—even *if* it's another mistake, even if both of us know it.

His lips crash against mine, heated and frantic, needy and desperate, as one hand cups my cheek and angles my head, and the other slides from my arm down across my hip to grip me there. He molds his body to mine, pressing me harder against the refrigerator, his tongue probing and seeking what both of us are looking for.

I wrap my arms around his neck, holding him to me, refusing to let him retreat even a fraction of an inch. Because if he does, it feels like I'll lose him forever. And even though I might not have any choice about that happening tomorrow, I'm not going to let it happen tonight.

Not when I can have this one more time with him.

His hand drops from my hip to between my legs, cupping me and sending a jolt of pleasure through me. I groan into his mouth and pull him impossibly closer, grinding down on his palm, ravenous for what my body needs.

This won't be slow and sweet; this will be how it always was after that deployment. It will be hard and fast. It will be all Chaos, but even if that's all I can get from him, I'll take it greedily.

I drop my hands from his neck to undo his jeans

and shove them down his hips as he continues to work me up. My arousal seeps through my thong and pants, almost embarrassingly wet for the man who always knew just how to touch me to make me fly on a cloud of bliss.

He pulls his hand away long enough to shove the material covering me down to my ankles, and I haphazardly try to kick them off while stroking his cock between us.

A low, rumbling groan falls from his lips against mine, and he rolls his hips, driving his length into my firm grip. He fucks my hand, his body seeking that which I'm more than willing to give.

His hands move to my hips, and he lifts me easily to wrap my legs around his waist and align him with my slick core. He drives up into me in one long, hard thrust, fulling impaling me on his dick and slamming me to the unyielding fridge behind me.

I cling to his neck, digging my nails into his nape and tightening my pussy around him. He moans and plunges into me again, hitting that spot that makes my mouth fall open on a gasp.

"Yes! God, Kalen...Please, just like that. Don't ever stop."

CHAOS

DON'T EVER STOP...

If we lived in a perfect world, I never would. I would fuck this woman to endless orgasms until we both die—content and in each other's arms, my dick still buried inside her for eternity.

But this isn't a perfect world.

It's a harsh reality.

One where we can never be together, where it isn't safe, where what we want must be ignored for what is *right.*

Christ, this feels right, though.

It always has with Avery.

From the moment she smiled at me in algebra, I knew I was a fucking goner for this woman. I got lost in her green eyes then, the same way I do now, like I'm surrounded by a forest full of towering pines engulfing me and preventing the outside world from invading.

All the threats, all the pain, all the lies and silent truths melt away.

Every drive of my hips cements me further inside her, secures the connection that's always been there even more. That can never be broken—not by time, not by distance, not by our best efforts to shatter it. Her cunt ripples around my cock, sucking me in deeper, begging me to stay inside her forever the same way her words did.

I would if I could.

Nothing has ever felt as good as her body cocooning mine. No sound as beautiful as our shared breaths and moans. No taste as addictive as her mouth or as divine as her cunt and release on my tongue.

Avery is *everything*, and I'll do anything for her—even die if that's what it takes to ensure she's safe. But in this moment, I can't think about what will happen in the next few days or what *might* happen after that. All that matters is her nails scoring the back of my neck, my name tumbling from her lips, the rolling of her hips to meet my thrusts, and the way she looks at me—the endless sea of green clouded with lust.

Her heels dig into my lower back, urging me forward, demanding I move faster and harder. She chases her release the same way I do the dregs of society, the people who think they have no one to answer to and do whatever they want regardless of the consequences or who gets hurt. I always succeed at my missions, and I refuse to fail when it comes to Avery.

The harder I ram into her, the more frantic she becomes, her nails biting into my neck, chest heaving against mine, breaths short and hot, her skin ablaze with the heat of our connection.

How did I ever walk away from this woman?

It's a stupid question, but one I can't stop from running endlessly through my head with every drive of my hips.

A beautiful, loyal, giving woman who never asked me for anything but to love her...

And I destroyed it because I had to.

Because I had no choice.

And I'll walk away again when all this is over. But I'll leave with the memory of *this*. Of being inside her again, of her cunt clasping me, drawing me inside her, of needing me the same way I do her.

Her mouth falls open, head dropped back against the fridge, tossing side to side. "Kalen, please, I can't..."

She can't get there.

The explosive releases we both seek are so close, within sight and reach, but she's holding back again, just as she did last night. She's fighting it, allowing something else to interfere.

Whether that be her fear of what will happen when we leave tomorrow, her knowledge that this will be the last time we're together, or whatever she and Viktoria were talking about that she refuses to tell me, it's keeping her from finding the bliss she seeks.

Moving my hand from her hip, I bring it to her face and grip her chin, holding it in place as I still inside her. "Open your eyes, Avery. Look at me."

Her lids flutter, and her lips part slightly on a frustrating groan. "Why did you stop?"

"Because you need to let go."

She shakes her head, tears shimmering in her eyes. "No, I can't. I—"

I drag my hips back slowly and then drive into her hard, ramming her against the fridge door. "Let. Go." I plunge into her again, using long, slow strokes. "Whatever it is. It isn't important. Not right now. Let." I thrust again. "It." Once more. "Go."

A tiny mewl falls from her lips, and a tear slowly descends on her pale cheek. "I can't. There's something you need to know. I should have—"

I silence her with a kiss, ending whatever confession she feels compelled to give me. There isn't anything she could say that would change the past or what has to happen in the future.

I'm leaving tomorrow, and I'm going to do whatever it takes to protect her. And right now, I'm going to do whatever it takes to make her come. So I can see that weight lift off her shoulders on a cloud of ecstasy and feel her pussy clenching on my cock.

I ghost my lips across hers softly, rolling and grinding my hips to hers, building the rhythm with languid strokes at just the right angle. "Just let it go, baby. For me. I want you to come for me."

"Oh, God..." Her lips tremble against mine, her hips moving faster, her hands clinging to my neck. "I can't, Kalen. I can't let you go. Not ever..."

Her words slice at my heart, making my strokes falter.

She doesn't mean it.

Not after all this time. Not after all the pain I've caused her. It's the adrenaline flooding her system, the combination of her trauma and her body being primed and ready to explode that made those words come from her lips.

Letting go is the only option.

For both of us.

So, I redouble my efforts, kissing her like she's my oxygen while I pound into her relentlessly, pinning her in place with my body and my desire to give her one moment of freedom from whatever haunts her.

I know all too well what living with ghosts is like.

She doesn't need to ever know that pain.

Someone as perfect as she is inside and out should only ever know hope and beauty.

And with one final thrust, she finally gasps and gives herself over to her release, her pussy rippling and clenching at my cock, pulling my own orgasm from deep inside.

I empty myself into her, spilling not only my cum but also all the things I wish I could tell her, all the agony I've lived with every day since we've been apart, the truths that can never be spoken. She jerks in my arms, her body spasming and her head dropping back as she rides out the wave of pleasure coursing through her.

She finally sags against me, burying her face into my neck, her warm breath tickling my already-heated skin. I wrap my arms around her, clutching her to me, holding her like I never will again.

Because there's a good chance I won't.

We're leaving for an almost-impossible mission tomorrow, and if I don't come back, I want to remember this moment as I take my final breath.

13

_____

CHAOS

For the first time since I became a professional soldier, my hand shakes. I switch my gun to my left hand for a moment to flex the right one, trying to stop the annoying quaking.

Reaper looks over at me, concern raising his brows. "You okay?"

No fucking way.

It would be impossible to be okay with everything that's going on.

I nod anyway. "Yeah."

He narrows his eyes on me but doesn't say anything else. And he doesn't have to. He sees right through my bullshit, just like he always could. Just like Avery always could.

She's the reason for all of this.

The reason we had to call in Cutter and Flash to

help. The reason we had to hop on that shitty little plane and sneak across the border armed to the fucking teeth. The reason my hand is shaking now.

Every mission I ever went on was important, essential, crucial for one reason or another. A move against a serious threat. Rescuing someone innocent. Protecting everyone back home. There was always a compelling reason for what we were doing. One that allowed me to pull the trigger without a second thought. But none of those reasons were ever so personal.

My action, my success or failure, never meant life or death to anyone I care about as much as I do Avery, which is why, for the first time in my life, my nerves feel fucking frayed, destroyed, utterly shot.

It has nothing to do with the fact that we're about to take on one of the nastiest cartels in Mexico or that we're doing it outnumbered. Over the last few days, Preacher and Cutter have been able to uncover more information about the men who control Merida, the ones connected to Perez, and all of it is wicked. These men don't play around, and they're armed to the teeth.

But none of that ever really mattered with any mission we went on. When it came down to getting the job done, we did it—short on supplies, short on men, somehow, we always managed. And we have to again— Avery's life depends on it.

"Does anyone have a visual on Perez?" I scan the open courtyard below me that's crawling with cartel men armed with ARs and looking ready for a fight.

The only things going for us are our superior

training and the fact that they will likely never antici-
pate that anyone will be stupid enough to attack them
on their home turf, to come to their compound and try
to stand against them.

"Negative."

"Negative."

Nothing from Cutter or Flash, and Mouth signals
no through the com, from their watch points, but it
doesn't mean the fucker isn't here. If he isn't outside,
then he has to be inside the main house or one of the
out buildings of the compound.

Preacher was able to use some of his sources to
confirm Perez returned to Merida in the last few days
and was seen heading out this way. Though the people
here don't want to talk about what goes on here. The
fear the cartel has instilled is very real. Taking them
out won't just help Avery; it will help the entire area.

All we have to do is get him in our crosshairs and
eliminate anyone else connected to this group who sets
foot on the compound.

The sun finally sinks below the horizon, casting the
entire valley into darkness. Spotlights blink to life
around the compound, illuminating the perimeter so
the cartel members can keep an eye on any potential
threats.

Two men at the massive, iron front gates stand
together, smoking a cigarette and chatting about something that has them both tossing their heads back and
laughing.

You won't be laughing much longer, fuckers.

From what we've been able to piece together from our recon over the last two days, as many as twenty-two men occupy and control the compound at any given time.

We've had worse odds.

I glance at my watch anxiously. The sooner this is over, the sooner we can get back and return to our normal lives—helping people by doing the only thing we're good at—this.

We may not be heroes, but we're all some people have, including Avery. I was all she ever had after her grandfather died. Between a non-existent father and drug-addicted mother, she didn't have anyone she could rely on, except me. I told her I would never leave, yet that's what I did. She may have been the one who filed those papers, but I was the one who forced her hand.

I didn't leave her a choice.

But it's a decision I'd make again and again to protect her because that's always going to be my job. Even if we're not married, even if we're not together. Even if we live on opposite sides of the country. I'll always watch out for her in any way I can, even if seeing her and not having her kills me slowly every day.

My watch clicks over to the designated time, and the shots ring out in perfect unison. All the flood-lights shatter and go black, and the men guarding the exterior succumb to bullets themselves. Between Mouth and Flash both taking aim, those men didn't stand a chance, and now, we have the benefit of darkness.

It's where we live, where we thrive, where I become Chaos.

Reaper, Cutter, Flash, and I descend toward the canyon, eyes locked on the various buildings, waiting for the resistance to emerge because these aren't the type of men who are going to go down without resistance.

That's okay. We enjoy the fight. It gets our blood pumping and makes us feel alive. We're ready to bring it to them. Any thoughts of Avery have been replaced by Chaos' absolute focus and need to destroy any threats.

I hustle with Reaper toward the main house, the most likely place Perez will be hiding, while Cutter and Flash clear the outbuildings and the rest of the compound with Mouth providing cover.

The house looms in front of us, a grand, opulent villa fit for a king, but according to Preacher, whoever is running this cartel has gone to great lengths to keep their identity hidden. Unusual considering most cartel heads flaunt their wealth and power publicly to keep people living in constant fear.

Whoever this guy is, he's now harboring our primary target, and no amount of firepower is going to keep us from bringing him to justice.

Reaper and I pause just outside the back kitchen door we've chosen as our entry point and wait. Humans are predictable, especially dumb ones, and most of the men in this cartel are just muscle, only here to intimidate and blindly pull the trigger when told. They'll come running straight to us now that they've heard the shots.

Heavy footsteps just inside the door confirm I'm right, and it flies open without any concern for what's on the other side. The second the first man steps through, I put a bullet through his temple while Reaper fires into his friend directly behind him.

They both drop to the ground, and we grab their weapons and move immediately past them, sweeping through the back hallway and toward the main portion of the house.

Gunfire sounds somewhere outside, likely Cutter and Flash in one of the other buildings.

Kitchen...clear.

Office...clear.

Living room...clear.

We head down the hallway toward the bedrooms, but something on the wall catches my eye, and I freeze. I signal for Reaper to stop and motion toward the photo of Perez with his arm around a familiar face.

Holy shit.

I clench my jaw and tighten my grip on my weapon.

We thought Perez wouldn't want his mistake known to the cartel because it would make him a target, but he doesn't have to worry about that. Because this is all in the family...

The cartel.

The house.

The land.

It all belongs to Perez and the man standing next to him who looks so much like him that they're certainly brothers and potentially even twins.

Now we've got two of them to worry about.

Fuck.

We make our way down the hall, clearing each empty bedroom until we finally reach a massive set of double doors that must lead to the master suite.

If he's here, that's the only place he can still be. I reach out to open the heavy wood separating us from our target, and gunfire tears through it. Reaper and I dive to the side, pressing our backs flat to the wall, but I'm not quick enough, and pain sears through my arm, the bullet embedding deep in the flesh.

Fuck.

Gritting my teeth, I check Reaper, who appears fine.

He nods toward my arm. "You okay?"

I nod.

Not really.

The pain spreads up my arm and through my shoulder, blood immediately flowing, but I push it to the back of my mind to focus on the threat on the other side of the now-destroyed door.

Reaper signals what he wants me to do, and we wait for the tell-tale sound of an empty magazine. Whoever is shooting has to reload, which gives us an opening.

We both turn toward the wood that now looks like Swiss cheese, and Reaper kicks it open in one hard motion. It shatters easily, and we fire without hesitation, Reaper taking the left side of the room, me the right.

I unleash a torrent of bullets at whoever might be in here. One man cries out and crumples to the floor. Two more drop, taking cover from our assault behind a massive bed in the center of the room, but now that they've had time to reload, Reaper and I advance and peg them off before they can fire again.

Three down.

I scan the space quickly for any other threats, but it's silent and empty save for the regal furnishings.

Where the hell is Perez?

Reaper follows me down a small hallway that must lead to the ensuite. A brief flash of movement to my left is the only warning I get before another bullet slams into me, hitting me square in the chest.

I stagger, the blow thankfully striking my vest. It knocks all the air from my lungs, but I return fire as I stumble back, my shoulders hitting the wall behind me. Reaper returns a single shot from my right and hits my assailant.

The man lands on the carpet inside the closet where he was hiding, and I struggle to suck in a breath, agony engulfing my chest and arm. Reaper enters the closet and stands over the guy, and I push my feet, still unable to breathe, and struggle over to them on shaking legs.

I'm not about to let a bullet stop me from getting to this fucker. Pushing Reaper out of the way, I brace myself against the doorjamb and stare down at the man on the floor.

He rolls over toward us, a bloody, sinister smile on his face. It could be Perez, or it could be his brother. Either way, it doesn't matter. Both need to go for this world to be rid of the true threats.

"You think you've won?" He shakes his head as blood bubbles from his lips, the gaping wound in his chest a definite death shot. "You haven't done anything."

I press my foot down onto his chest, directly over the wound, ensuring the most pain possible. "Who are you?"

He tries to laugh, but all that comes out is a strangled, gurgling sound. "The question is...who are *you?*" He coughs up more blood and shifts uncomfortably under my foot. "You're too late, Kalen Riggs."

My name coming from his lips makes Reaper and me freeze.

"How the hell do you know my name?"

A slow grin spreads across his crimson lips. "You aren't the only one with powerful friends, Mr. Riggs. Friends who can find anyone, anywhere. Even your ex-wife."

"Fuck."

AVERY

VIKTORIA PEEKS out the window again, staring at the quiet street, chewing on her lip, her foot bouncing up and down. "Something's wrong."

Pulling my knees to my chest on the recliner, I hug them close and rest my head on them, watching the woman who is usually so calm slowly start to unravel. "I thought I was the one who was supposed to be unnecessarily nervous."

She looks at me with a furrowed brow and shakes her head. "This isn't unnecessarily." Her eyes dart to her watch, her lips twisting into a frown. "We should have heard from them by now."

The last two days have been pure agony waiting for a word from Reaper and Kalen—nothing but pacing and worrying and imagining every horrific scenario possible. It's hard not knowing what they're walking into and going up against.

I've done my best to try not to overthink it, to remain calm and trust that Kalen will make it back like he promised.

He said it would take a few days for them to do their recon and go in, so we really don't have any reason to be worried yet—at least, that's what I keep telling myself. "Maybe they don't have anything to update us with?"

Vik shakes her head. "No. Reaper has been texting me updates every few hours, and he said they were going in tonight and would get in touch with me before they got on the plane to head back."

I check the clock on the microwave. "It's only midnight. Maybe they got held up?"

She chews on her cheek, letting the blinds fall closed and wandering back toward me. "You know I'm not one to overreact, but after what happened with them when we were in New York, I'm a little leery about this whole *going up against an entire cartel* thing."

"What happened in New York?"

For all I know about Kalen, his life over the last four years is a complete mystery to me, and I haven't had the guts to ask him about it. Whatever Vik is referencing seems important, though, and God knows Kalen will likely never tell me a word of it.

Vik paces the room, continually glancing at her phone on the counter. "Reaper, Mouth, Chaos, and I took down a Russian human trafficking ring."

"You *what*?"

She offers a humorless smile. "Yeah, it's a long story, but needless to say, I witnessed first-hand what the guys are capable of, but I also saw Reaper almost die. He barely made it out of that mission alive, and these aren't some local thugs they're up against." Vik pauses, offering a half-smile. "I'm really trying to stop myself from having a total meltdown."

"You don't think something happened, do you?"

Her lips pressed together in a firm line, she shakes her head. "I don't know." She sucks in a deep breath. "No.

They're fine. They're professionals. They know what to do and how to do it. I just have to trust they're okay and there's some valid reason Reaper hasn't gotten in touch yet."

"Yes, do that." I give her what I hope is a reassuring smile. "I know it's hard when you're worrying about someone you love."

Vik nods slowly. "Reaper and I are...complicated." She laughs lightly. "Though, not nearly as complicated as you and Chaos."

"Isn't that the truth?" I sigh and lean back in the chair, letting my eyes drift closed. Barely sleeping for days is taking its toll, but I know I won't be able to until I'm confident they're all safe.

"Have you given any more thought to talking to Chaos when he gets back?"

She doesn't need to clarify *what* I should be talking to him about. The last few days have given me time to completely come clean to Viktoria about what I've been keeping from Kalen...and to explain why.

"It's all I've been able to think about. It gives me something else to obsess over other than my worry."

Her humorless laugh fills the small apartment. "Oh, God, aren't we a pair?"

"You know why I can't ever tell him..."

It's the same debate I've been having in circles—both with myself and with Vik since the guys left. If Kalen comes out of this alive, I can't destroy him with the truth. It would be too painful for him to overcome.

"I think you need to give him some credit and trust he can handle it."

"Like you need to trust that they're okay and will call when they can?"

A grin tugs at her lips. "Touché."

Almost as if in answer to my comment, her phone rings and vibrates across the counter. She rushes the last few steps and grabs it while I hold my breath.

"Reaper...what's the status?"

She turns back to me, her eyes wide.

I shift upright, my entire body tensing, seeing the panic in her gaze. "What's wrong?"

Holding up a hand to silence me, she shakes her head. "Okay." She hustles toward the window and peeks out the blinds again. "I understand." She ends the call, slides her phone into her pocket, and stares at the street in front of the repair shop. "Get your shoes on."

"What?" A chill spreads over my skin, instantly eliminating the confidence I tried to hold so tightly only moments ago. "What do you mean?"

"Get your shoes on." Her words come out sharp, like an order from a cop, not a request from a friend. "Now!"

I shake my head, trying to figure out what's happening as she pulls her gun from the holster at her hip. "What's going on?"

She snaps her head toward me. "Get your fucking shoes on. We have to *go*."

"Go?" I push up from the chair, my legs shaking. My heart stops as I try to process what's happening. "Go where? What the hell is going on?"

Viktoria flicks off the safety on her gun and checks the window. "They guys are on their way to the plane right now, but they think Perez knows where you are."

"What? How is that possible?"

I was supposed to be *safe* here. Kalen said there was no way this place could be traced to him, even if anyone ever connected us.

How could Ricardo have found me here?

Viktoria shakes her head. "I don't know. They just said to get the fuck out. So, that's what we're doing. We'll figure it out later."

"Oh, God..." I press my hand over my mouth to keep myself from vomiting. "Are they okay? Are they meeting us somewhere?"

She rushes toward the kitchen, grabs her keys off the counter, and heads back toward the window. "Shoes. *Now*!"

Shoes.

Get shoes.

I stumble on unsteady feet toward the bedroom, grab my shoes from the floor just inside the door, and slip them on as I approach her near the window. It hasn't gone unnoticed that she didn't respond to my question. "Answer me, Viktoria. Are they okay?"

Her hard gaze meets mine for a second. "Kalen has been shot."

It's the second time I've heard those words. The first time was the beginning of the end of our marriage, and now, it feels like I'm about to lose him completely.

The room tunnels around me, my vision going

black around the edges, and I stumble forward and press my hand to the wall to stop from falling over. "Oh, my God...is he..."

She shakes her head. "I don't know. We can't worry about that right now. It's out of our control. I have to get you out of here. You're my primary concern."

"But—"

Her hand tightens around my arm. "No *buts*. Move." She motions for me to head toward the door but then freezes. "Shit."

"What is it?"

Viktoria's body stiffens, her laser focus down at the street. "We're about to have company that doesn't look too friendly."

Bullets tear through the front of the window, shattering the glass and throwing fragments at us. Viktoria lunges toward me, knocking me to the floor and covering me with her body.

Another volley of bullets punches through the wall and soar through the now-open window, slamming into the opposite side of the room, tearing into Kalen's chair and the kitchen counter.

My heart thunders against my ribs, my ears ringing from the shots.

Vik pushes on my back. "Stay down."

"Wh-what do we do?"

She crawls back toward the window and reaches up to fire out. "Go into the bedroom. See if you can get out the window."

"What? I can't leave you!"

"Yes, you can!" She glares at me, then turns and fires off a few more rounds toward whoever is outside. "If you can't get out, you *hide* like your damn life depends on it."

Pushing aside the fear threatening to paralyze me, I scramble across the worn wooden floor, staying as low as I can, tears streaming down my face, blurring my vision. My hand hits the bedroom door. I nudge it open and crawl inside, slamming the door behind me before I reach up with a shaking hand and flip the lock.

Don't ever lock that fucking door again.

Kalen's voice rings in my ears, and a sob climbs up my throat. I clamp my hand over my mouth and scan the room. The window is far too small for me to fit out of, and the mattress rests on the floor—no bed to hide under.

My eyes land on Kalen's footlocker. Without even thinking, I race over to it, throw it open, and freeze. A photo of us sits atop his clothes, our much-younger, smiling faces staring back at me as if to taunt me with the time when we were so naïve and hopeful.

He has to be okay.

He has to come back to me.

I shove the stack of clothes to the side to make room, then climb in and curl up inside the tight space, resting my head on the shirts that used to bring me so much comfort, heavy with his scent. This has held Kalen's personal possessions since the day he enlisted, the only place he keeps the things most important to him. And now, it's my only hope to save my own life.

My fingers curl around the picture frame, and I clutch it to my chest, slapping my other hand over my mouth to stop myself from crying out in a way that might give away where I'm hiding.

The gunfire stops—the only sounds, my own breathing and the blood rushing in my ears. I strain to hear anything else through the closed box, any clues about what might be happening to Vik in the living room.

Sharp cracks...gunshots.

Closer this time.

Vik!

I bite back the sob and squeeze my eyes closed, willing myself to remain silent. Holding my breath, I wait in the pitch-black confines of what might become my coffin.

Heavy footsteps...

A loud bang, the bedroom door being broken down...

Indistinguishable words in Spanish...

I continue to hold my breath, clinging to the photo like I am my hope that Kalen is all right.

Please, God, let them just go...

The lid jerks opens, and I lash out with the picture frame, the only weapon I have, but strong hands reach down to grab me and jerk me to my feet.

A split second later, the world goes dark again.

14

AVERY

The world around me slowly comes back into focus. Hazy light breaking through the darkness, but with it comes pain. A constant throbbing in my right temple unlike anything I've ever felt before. Wincing, I try to reach up for it, but the sharp bite of something binding my hands behind me digs into my wrists.

"What the hell?" My voice comes out rough and tortured, like I've been drinking gravel or screaming endlessly.

I open my eyes slowly, my vision fuzzy and the room around me tilting as if on a ship riding vicious waves on an unsettled ocean. Flashes of beige carpet. An unfamiliar dark wooden bed. Brown drapes over a tall window.

Where the hell am I?

"Good morning, Avery." Ricardo's familiar voice jerks me fully awake and back to the present. "You've been out for quite a while."

The memories of what happened last night come flooding back, threatening to overwhelm me at once, and I twist my neck, scanning the unfamiliar room and trying to find him.

He leans against a doorframe to my right, watching me with a smug tilt of his lips, arms crossed over his chest, in his usual pristine white dress shirt and perfectly pressed black slacks.

It's the same thing he wore every day—always well-dressed, always poised, always *perfect*.

How did I not see it?

How did I not know what he was doing?

I swallow through my dry, scratchy throat. "What do you want? Where's Vik?"

He raises a dark eyebrow. "Is that the other woman at your husband's place? I'm pretty sure she's bled out by now."

No!

The nonchalance with which he says the words twist a knife into my gut, and I gasp against the physical pain. New tears fall on my cheeks, and I shake my head, squeezing my eyes shut, refusing to accept what he says as true. "No, she's can't be. She can't…"

Ricardo pushes off the doorjamb and slowly walks toward me, casually, like he didn't just admit to having Viktoria killed on top of everything else I know he's done.

This man is a monster, one disguised as a caring, upstanding family man with a thriving business that helps immigrants and those struggling to make their American dreams come true.

I never knew what evil looked like until today, until I saw the man I used to eat lunch across from, used to laugh with, used to *trust*, look back at me with such blank disinterest. Ricardo doesn't care what happens to me. I'm nothing more than an obstacle to him—one to be removed by any means necessary.

He stops in front of me and offers me the same smile he has for years. His hard eyes soften slightly, and he shakes his head and *tsks*. "It really is too bad you and Amelia stumbled upon what you did. You always did a very good job for me."

"What do you want? Why haven't you just killed me? You've already tried."

He nods slowly. "I'm impressed you got away from Manuel. He's very good at his job, but you outsmarted him." A grin spreads across his lips. "Impressive. Did you learn that from your husband?"

"Ex-husband."

"Right." He grins again. "I saw the divorce decree when I was digging into your background, trying to figure out where you might have run off to after you saw what you did." He paces in front of me, hands crossed behind his back. "You have cost me a lot of good men."

"Why did you kill Amelia?"

"Come now, Avery." Ricardo shakes his head. "I

couldn't let her keep digging into where the money was coming from. You and I both know that."

I release a sob and drop my head. "You didn't have to kill her."

He squats in front of me and lifts my chin with a firm finger. "I did. But as soon as I get some answers from you, you'll see her again."

His words slowly click in my head.

"That's why you haven't killed me...you *need* something from me."

He smiles again. "Your ex-husband and his friends have caused me a lot of trouble over the last few days. I need all their names. Ways to find them. Because I'm certain they're smart enough not to go back to his place now that we discovered it—which wasn't easy, by the way. It took days of analyzing red light camera footage to figure out what vehicles were in the area of *South of the Border* before it was destroyed, then following them around town via other cameras to narrow down a location."

That's how they found Kalen's place.

We underestimated Ricardo and his resources. Preacher is our computer wizard, but it seems Ricardo has at least one of his own helping him in this sinister endeavor.

I refuse to give him anything that will assist him, no matter *what* he threatens to do to me. "I'm not telling you anything."

Ricardo chuckles and shakes his head. "They all say that, but let me tell you something, Avery. Everyone, and I mean *everyone,* talks, even the most well-trained men from some of the most violent families." A softness overtakes his gaze, and for a split second, I see the man I have known all these years. "I don't want to have to do it, Avery, but I will do what I must to get you to talk."

I have no doubt he means it and will inflict serious pain to get what he wants, but I'm willing to endure anything to protect the guys. "I don't know anything. Honestly. He always kept me in the dark to protect me."

He nods slowly. "Smart man, but you probably know more than you think you do, and once I'm confident I have all the information you can offer me, I'll end your suffering."

"They'll come for me, you know."

A low, dark laugh rumbles in his chest. "They'll never find you here."

Footsteps sound in the hallway just outside the bedroom, and a man enters the room, stoic, holding a phone. "Sir, something's happened at the compound."

Perez stands, looks at me without saying a word, and moves to the hall, putting his back to me. He speaks with someone on the phone, his body stiffening. When he turns back to me, he's a completely different man.

Eyes now cold and emotionless.

Body tense.

Fists at his sides.

This is the *true* Ricardo Perez. The part of himself

he managed to conceal from me, from Amelia, from his own wife and children.

"Your ex-husband and his friends killed my brother in Mexico. Someone was just able to get word to me." His words vibrate with his anger. "I was just there, meeting with him to coordinate a response to the trouble you've caused. They only missed me by hours."

"Shitty luck."

His fist lashes out and slams into my jaw, snapping my head back and stealing my breath. I gasp, trying to suck in a breath through the agony, and he squats in front of me, jaw tight, flexing out the hand he just struck me with.

"Now, you are going to tell me everything you know. No more games. No more pleasantries. The time for all that has long passed."

CHAOS

THE CAR HITS A POTHOLE, jerking me violently across the back seat, and I grimace and grit my teeth against the pain threatening to make me black out. "Watch how you fucking drive, asshole. We barely got out of Mexico alive, and now, you're trying to kill me on the fucking way home."

Reaper glances at me in the rearview mirror, his jaw hard. "Shut up. If I *could* go any faster, I *would*, even if it fucking killed you."

He barrels through a red light, and a car lays on its horn, slamming its brakes to avoid T-boning us in the intersection.

"She's still not answering?"

Slipping in and out of consciousness since Reaper called Viktoria hours ago from Mexico has left me at a bit of a disadvantage in terms of knowing what the fuck is going on. I don't even know how long it's been since we landed.

He shakes his head. "She's not picking up."

The agony I feel matches what his words hold.

That fucker in Mexico said my name. He knew who I was and who Avery was to me, which means she and Viktoria are in danger. Not being able to get in touch with them during the agonizingly slow flight back has ratcheted up the tension on top of the fact that I seem intent on bleeding to death before we ever find them.

I push myself into a sitting position, and everything spins around me. Blood trickles down my arm despite the tourniquet and temporary patch we did on our way to the shitty airstrip we used to enter and leave Mexico.

Mouth turns back to look at me from the front passenger seat, a single eyebrow raised.

"I'm alive. That's all I got right now."

He nods and returns his focus to Reaper's phone in his hand, redialing Viktoria every few minutes as we try to make it back to my place.

The light in front of us turns red, and the cross-traffic speeds through the intersection in front of us.

Reaper slams on the brakes, unable to make it across the sea of vehicles without killing all of us.

He punches his fist into the dashboard. "Why the fuck isn't she answering?"

"Maybe they're somewhere she can't. Hiding."

It's wishful thinking, but it's the only thing preventing me from either letting myself float off into the darkness threatening to encroach from all sides or to push Reaper out of that driver's seat and gun it straight through that traffic to try to find Avery.

If I didn't believe Viktoria would die before letting anything happen to Avery, I never would have left her. The fact that we can't reach them makes me heave again in the backseat.

The ring of Reaper's phone in Mouth's hand makes me jerk my head back up, and Mouth hands it to Reaper.

Reaper brings the phone to his ear, free hand tightening on the wheel. "Vik?" He listens for a moment, then his eyes widen. "What? Where is she? Is she okay?" He glances at both of us, panic in his gaze. "Okay, I'll be right there."

He ends the call, handing the phone back to Mouth. "That was Johns Hopkins. Viktoria was brought in with three gunshot wounds."

I shift forward slightly. "Fuck..."

"She's alive, but..."

"Avery?"

He shakes his head. "They brought her in alone. The woman at the hospital made the call from Vik's phone. She said she just dialed back the number she saw had been calling repeatedly. She doesn't know anything other than Viktoria was brought in and is being treated."

A vise tightens around my chest, making it impossible to breathe.

Reaper's knuckles whiten on the wheel. "We have to get to the hospital."

"No." I shake my head, trying to clear the panic and haze from blood loss. "I have to know what happened to Avery. She's..."

I can't even say the words.

She's everything to me...

If anything happens to her, it will spell the end for me. There wouldn't be anything left, no reason to keep going, to keep fighting for what's right.

The light turns green, and Reaper floors it. "We drive past your place to see what's going on, then go straight to the hospital."

I hold my breath the rest of the drive there, unable to think, unable to feel, unable to do anything but picture Avery's lifeless body lying on the floor of my shitty apartment.

Reaper remains stoic and silent, and the closer we get to my street, the more tense I become, which only makes my arm hurt more and my heart threaten to stop beating with every passing block. Squad cars line the road ahead, preventing anyone from turning down toward my place.

I lean forward slightly, resting my good arm on the

edge of Mouth's seat. "I need to know what happened up there."

Reaper pulls to the curb well short of the road-block. "I need to get to Viktoria."

Mouth glances between us, and I nod at him.

"Get out. See what information you can get. Text us as soon as you know anything."

He nods and jumps from the car, jogging up to the roadblock and then slowing down to walk casually toward the officers as Reaper makes a right-hand turn.

I relax back into my seat and dig into my bag on the floor for my gun. "I'm not going to the hospital with you."

Reaper glances at me in the rearview. "What?"

"I'm going after him."

He scowls at me. "You can barely sit up straight. You're not going after anyone."

I cinch the tourniquet around my arm even tighter. "I've got a few more hours before this gets lethal. I can't walk into the hospital with you like this, anyway."

"Shit." Reaper rubs at his nape with one hand and locks his gaze with mine in the mirror. "You don't want to wait for backup?"

"Go take care of your woman, and I'll go find mine."

My phone vibrates in my pocket, and I wince, shifting to my side to pull it out. "It's Mouth."

No coroner van.

A tiny bit of the weight threatening to crush my chest lifts. "He says there isn't a coroner van."

Reaper releases a relieved sigh. "So, she's not..."

"No."

At least, not yet.

If Perez's men went into my place intent on killing her, she would be dead. Which means, he wants something from her; he has some reason for keeping her alive—probably temporarily.

Police will only say it was a shooting. Single victim.

"Cops are saying single victim shooting."

Reaper nods. "So, Avery was gone before the cops got there. Do you think she got away?"

I shake my head. "I'd love to believe that, but I don't think so. She would have tried to find a way to get in touch with us, would have left us a message somehow. I think Perez's guys took her."

"Where?"

"Fuck if I know, but I do know where I can start. Give me the list."

Reaper peeks at me over his shoulder. "The list?"

I nod, and he leans over and pops the glove compartment, pulling out the list Preacher gave us of every property connected to Perez. *South of the Border* is already up in smoke, as is the warehouse where Perez did most of his dirty work. That scratches two addresses off the list, but it leaves almost a dozen others.

"I'll start with places he's most likely to take her, the businesses that aren't open or buildings that are remote, then work my way down the list." I squeeze

Reaper's shoulder. "Text me with any updates once you see Vik."

He nods. "Drop me at the hospital and have Mouth come meet you."

I shake my head. "No, you need Mouth there watching the hospital in case they come for Viktoria again."

Reaper snarls at me, anger flashing in his eyes. "You can't go after them alone."

"I can, and I will. I'm getting Avery back, no matter what."

15

CHAOS

L a Cantina doesn't look any different than any of the other restaurants or buildings I've already visited and lit up tonight, trying to find Avery.

Trying...and failing.

Where the fuck are they?

Perez must have her *somewhere*, and this is the final building on the list from Preacher. If she isn't here...

No.

I can't even think that. If I start considering that possibility, my focus will be shot, and the belief that I will find her is the only thing keeping me from dropping to the fucking ground right now.

My body threatens to betray me, to give out when I'm determined to keep going. It's only happened one other time, and that was when my whole world went to shit. When I destroyed my life with Avery, when I blew up her world.

That won't happen again.

I refuse to fail tonight, refuse to fail *her*. Even if I have to crawl into this damn building and fight Perez with my one good arm, I'll fucking do it.

There isn't any other option *but* to succeed.

I climb from the car, wincing at the agony now engulfing the entire left side of my body, my arm essentially useless, hanging at my side. Physical pain, I can live with, but the thought of losing her, of *anything* happening to her, is far too much to bear.

Reaper must be completely losing his shit right now, waiting for word on Viktoria. Sitting at the hospital, helpless, while surgeons try to save her life. Perez will pay for what he did to her, just like he will for everything he's put Avery through. And if he's harmed one fucking hair on her head, I will rip his balls off and shove them down his throat until he chokes on them.

But I have to find the fucker first.

The building remains dark, the only lights small green dots on the cameras outside, facing the parking lot and street. They'll know I'm here, but it doesn't matter at this point. After what I've already done to all the other locations on the list, they have to know I'm coming.

It's been closed for hours, the employees long gone. Either Perez has her in there, or his men will be waiting to ambush me.

I make my way around the back, carrying my bag

over my good shoulder, and disconnect the power to the building. Each step across the parking lot toward the rear entrance takes every ounce of strength I have left, but I manage to set the charge on the door and blow it, gaining entry.

Smoke still fills the air as I enter, gun ready, and scan the rear hallway and kitchen as I set the charges necessary to bring this place down.

Empty.

Storage room.

Empty.

Bathrooms.

Empty.

The entire fucking building...

Empty.

Just like my heart is knowing Avery's being held by that asshole and I can't find them. I've literally burned down his world, looking for her, destroyed everything, even killed his brother, and still, the thing that's most important to me is in his sick, twisted hands.

The room starts to spin, my vision blurring around the edges—no sleep and exertion over the last several days, combined with the blood loss and likely infection, create sheer havoc on my body.

I slowly lower myself to the tile floor of the kitchen and rest my head back against the fridge, releasing a long groan. Perez and his men may not have been waiting for me, but by now, they know I've taken out the rest of the restaurants and why.

All I have to do is wait, and soon rather than later, they'll come.

My phone buzzes in my pocket, and I lean to the side and pull it out to read the text from Reaper.

She's still in surgery. Might be a few more hours. Anya is on her way here.

Hell.

At least she's alive, though.

There's a chance.

Hope.

All I have is blind faith that Avery's alive and I can get to her in time.

I open my bag and ensure everything's ready for when Perez's men finally show up, and I fight the desire of my heavy eyelids to drift closed, instead focusing on the last few days with Avery.

It took her falling into something this bad to finally reach out to me because I hurt her so badly. She felt like she couldn't, *shouldn't* contact me, no matter how bad things may have been over the last four years. I had no idea how much she's been suffering. With all the harsh realities staring me in the face at that time, I thought what I did was right for her.

And I still do.

Once she's safe, I'll make sure she's far away from any form of danger again, even me. I'll get her set up somewhere new. Peaceful. Quiet. Somewhere she can restart her life without the pain I cause, where there isn't any chance she'll run afoul of anyone like Perez again.

Then, maybe, I can sleep, knowing she's safe.

The sound of an engine in the parking lot jerks me from my thoughts, and I tighten my grip on the weapon, waiting for whatever will be walking through that door.

Three car doors open and close outside, followed by hurried footsteps across the asphalt. As soon as the men round the corner of the building and step into the open doorway, I fire, taking out two with shots to the chest.

Where's the third?

I struggle to my feet and creep over to the door, checking to ensure they're not getting up. Kicking their weapons away, I press my back against the wall immediately to the side of the threshold and wait. Another minute passes, then another, before light footsteps finally move toward me.

Come on, fucker.

The man pauses just outside, looking down at his friends. He cautiously steps over their bodies to enter, gun held out in front of him. I fire one shot into his hand, and the weapon immediately tumbles on top of the bodies.

He cries out, and I wrap my good arm around his neck, transferring my weapon to the other while ignoring the pain the movement causes. I drag him back, applying pressure on his windpipe and airway. He claws at me with his one good hand, the other hanging at his side, half of it blown off, blood dripping onto the tile.

I press my back against the wall and crank on his neck harder, fighting my desire to end him immediately. That will get me nowhere.

"Where is she?"

The man gasps for air, twisting his head to try to relieve the tension on his airway. "Don't...know..."

I crank my arm tighter. "Where. Is. She?"

His legs start to give out, and I ease up slightly before he passes out and is of no use to me. "I-I don't know who you're talking about."

Fucking liar.

"I can make this very painful for you"—I retighten my hold, pressing on his airway and artery—"until I get the information I want."

He tries to scream, attempts to plead for his life, but all that comes out are gasps and indistinguishable words.

"Tell me where your boss is."

His body stiffens slightly. He *might* not know who Avery is or where she is, but he knows where the man himself is, and if I find Perez, I'll find her.

"Tell me."

"A house." He swallows thickly against my arm. "Down on Umbra..."

"That's all I needed to know."

I force my almost dead arm up, press the barrel to his temple, and pull the trigger. He immediately goes limp in my arms, and I drop it unceremoniously like a rag doll, step over it, and grab my bag. Without a second look at the corpses, I step over them and walk away from *La Cantina* with renewed energy and hope.

That and adrenaline are the only things keeping me going at this point.

I hustle to the SUV, start it, and press the detonator switch for the charges I set inside. The place erupts, flames leaping into the dark sky, the bodies of Perez's men engulfed along with the last vestiges of his business here in the area.

Now all that's left is him.

AVERY

MY ENTIRE BODY SHAKES, my teeth rattling together as I fight passing out again. The coppery tang of blood fills my mouth from my split lip. I gag on it and spit it onto the carpet under the chair where the madman I once trusted implicitly has me restrained.

Ricardo looms over me, his hands fisted at his sides, ready to strike again. I squeeze my eyes shut, trying to get the room to stop spinning. He's hit me so many times already that I've lost count, and I can't watch it coming at me again.

But instead of another blow, he tilts my face up to him with an almost gentle hand at my chin. "You know I don't like having to do this, Avery. Just tell me what I need to know, and it can all be over."

I struggle to form words, my breath coming short

and sharp. "I only have one thing to tell you." I swallow and lock eyes with him. "Fuck you."

His strike comes swift and without warning, his heavy fist slamming into my cheek and sending my head snapping back. I gasp at the pain searing through my face and swallow the bile rising in my throat.

"I don't think you appreciate your situation, Avery."

"I told you...I don't know anything about any of Kalen's friends, about what their plans are, or where to find them."

It feels like we've been at this for hours. He keeps asking, and I keep giving him the same answer while my body only gets more bruised and battered.

He grips my chin tightly in his fingers. "I don't like having to hit a woman, Avery. This can all be over if you just come clean."

"I don't know anything." I keep repeating the same words, over and over, but he doesn't believe me. "I don't know *anything*."

Probably because I'm lying.

Kalen worked with those guys for a long time, and over the years we were together, I learned lots of information about them. Plenty of things that would be useful for someone like Ricardo, someone trying to get to them, but I'll be damned if I give any of it to him.

I'm not going to put them in the line of fire any more than I already have. They've already risked their lives for me multiple times and are already facing jail time or worse if they get caught. I won't put them in any more danger than they're already in by having this madman know anything personal about any of them. But maybe there's something I *can* tell him that will buy some time, keep me alive long enough for the guys to find me.

"I-I don't know anything about them. I swear. But I'll give you something else, something even more dangerous to you."

One of his thick, dark brows rises. "What's that?"

"The zip drive Amelia made with everything she found."

His jaw tightens. "She saved everything?"

I nod slowly. "Yes, and I'll tell you where it is. Just... can I have some water, please?"

It isn't the first time I've asked for it, but an almost-kind smile spreads across his lips, as if he's actually considering giving it to me this time to ease my dry, cracked lips and bruised body instead of keeping me miserable, thirsty, and at his will.

A hint of softness touches his dark eyes, and he turns back and inclines his head to his men who have been standing near the door, watching him torture me for who knows how long. One of them disappears down the hall, and Ricardo releases my face, letting my head drop and hang since I no longer have the power to hold it up.

Ricardo paces in front of me, body tense and only growing more so the longer we're in here, almost like he's waiting for something to happen, anticipating some news.

His man returns with a bottle of water. Ricardo

twists off the cap, lifts my chin, and holds it to my lips. I drink at it greedily, the cold water pouring down my neck and chest, the icy coolness welcome even though it stings against my injured mouth.

He pulls the bottle away, recaps it, and sets it on the floor near his feet. "Now, let's chat, like we used to back at the office."

I snort at the absurdity of the statement. "Like we used to? Before I knew you? You want to pretend I don't know what kind of a monster you really are now? That I haven't figured out what you've done? How many lives you've ruined."

His already-dark eyes go almost obsidian, his jaw hardening. "You have no idea what I've done or what I'm capable of."

The chill that spreads through me has nothing to do with the shock my body is going into and everything to do with the threat implicit in his words.

"What about your wife, your kids? How can you do this when you have a family?"

It's what I always wanted, what I always thought I would have eventually with Kalen, and Ricardo is lying to them, putting them at risk by playing this dangerous game.

He sneers at me. "I'm doing this *for* them. I built this empire with my brother to provide for both of our families, to ensure we could give them everything we never had as children."

"By selling drugs? By laundering money? By killing people with poison they put in their veins?"

"Their choice."

"Is that how you sleep at night? By telling yourself that?"

His expression hardens, and a sly smile overtakes his lips. "I sleep on a very expensive bed, in very expensive sheets, sometimes next to my beautiful wife who trusts me and loves me, sometimes next to an expensive whore who does the things my wife never would, and I never have trouble sleeping."

"You're a monster."

"And what does that make your ex-husband, hmm? After what *he's* done over the last few days?"

His question makes me bite back my continued tirade, not because I think Kalen or the guys are monsters, but rather because I don't want to defend them and unwittingly give away any information Ricardo could use to hurt them.

He shakes his head, rising to pace in front of me. "You know, I looked into both of you after you saw us in the warehouse and got away from Manuel, and it's incredible how little there is to find. Given what he's demonstrated the last few days, I'd wager a guess he's former military, likely a SEAL, maybe a Ranger or Delta Force."

I steel my expression so I don't give away how close he is to the truth.

"His skills have certainly served him well, but if he continues this war against me, he's going to see the true power of my organization. Hopefully, he already has."

What the hell does that mean?

A grin plays at his lips, like he knows something I don't. Whatever it is, he finds it excessively amusing, and that threatens to make me gag on my own fear again.

"You see, your ex-husband and his friends have been playing a dangerous game, making their way across town tonight and destroying all my properties, but it means we know where they're going. And eventually, my men are going to catch up with them. When they do, they're not going to be as kind to them as I have been to you." Ricardo squats in front of me again, taking the bottle of water back into his hands. "Now, why don't you tell me about the zip drive."

Over my dead fucking body.

A phone rings in the hallway, and one of Ricardo's men pulls it from his pocket and answers. He glances back at Ricardo with wide eyes.

Ricardo rises to his feet. "What? Did they get them?"

His man shakes his head. "*La Cantina* just exploded, and we haven't heard from Erik, Jorge, or Miguel."

"Fucking how?" Ricardo chucks the water bottle against the wall, his face reddening, hands fisting at his sides. "Fucking *how* does he keep doing this?"

Before I can stop it, a laugh slips between my split lips and fills the room.

Ricardo whirls around and glares at me. "You think this is funny? What he's doing?"

I shake my head, unable to drop the smile. "No, I think it's funny that he's coming for you and you think you can escape him. When he finds you, I can't wait to see what he does to you."

In one smooth motion, he pulls out a gun and points it against my forehead, pressing the barrel into my skin. "Will he think it's funny when he finds you with a bullet through your fucking head?"

Knowing Kalen and the guys have outsmarted Ricardo's plans thus far gives me a strange sense of power. "You're the one who's going to end up with a bullet in his head."

Ricardo acts so fast that I don't even realize he's moving his hand until the gun strikes me in the temple and pain sears through my vision, blinding me. I try to take a breath, but the pain robs me of it, and vomit finally makes its way up my throat that I barely manage to swallow back before he hits me again.

Everything goes dark.

16

CHAOS

The quaint bungalow sits quietly, just like all the others on the street. It should house some happy family, asleep in their beds, dreaming of school plays and what they need to accomplish at work tomorrow, but instead, the man I'm here to destroy and the woman I still love wait inside.

Unlike his places of business, no cameras film the outside of the house. Either this is a new purchase, or he never expected anyone to ever find it. Even Preacher didn't with his extensive ability to locate information on just about anything.

That's good—it means they'll never see me coming.

I'd love to have more time to properly recon the place, but neither Avery nor I have that luxury. I've been bleeding for more than twelve hours, and the sun is coming up far too soon, which means the neighborhood will be coming to life.

There's only one way to go in, and that's full fucking tilt. I'm not about to give anyone in there any warning or long enough to prepare themselves for what's coming.

I grab the grenade from my bag—its familiar weight in my hand almost like finding an old friend—and my lips curl slightly despite the situation. Perez and his men have greatly underestimated the lengths I will go to protect Avery, and I will use that to my every advantage.

With my bag of tricks slung over my good shoulder, I'm ready for these fuckers. Ready for anything they could ever throw at me.

I ready my weapon. Pull the pin, release the spoon, and toss the grenade at the front door.

4...3...2...1...

It blows it wide open, and I storm in through the smoke, firing three shots into the man on the floor immediately inside while he's still stunned by the blast.

I sweep in through the front hallway, past the stairs leading up, and into the kitchen. Empty takeout containers and remnants of what must have been dinner last night still litter the table. Enough for at least three people—Perez, this fucker, and probably one more.

And they know I'm here now.

I've lost the element of surprise, which makes this

even more dangerous for Avery. I have to take out those fuckers without hurting her, and she could be anywhere in this damn house.

Standing still, I listen for any signs of movement. Floorboards creak above me, but that doesn't mean someone isn't waiting to ambush me on this level. I make my way down the short hall to the two small bedrooms before returning to the stairs.

An ominous silence falls over the house, and the hairs on the back of my neck stand on end, a shiver rolling through me.

This isn't good.

I pause with my back to the wall just at the bottom of the stairwell, where I'm protected from exposure to anyone at the top of the flight. He'll be ready to fire the moment he hears me coming up, but that's just a risk I have to take if I want any chance of getting out of here with Avery.

Failure isn't an option in this mission.

If I don't push and do everything in my power to get her back, that man *will* kill her.

That means shoving aside the exhaustion, the pain, the desire of my body to just fall to the floor right now. I square my shoulders and move for the stairwell again.

Bullets tear into the floor and the wall immediately next to me, and I slide back and take cover again. He has the high ground, which is going to make this a lot more difficult.

I would kill to be able to have Mouth and Reaper

here now, but at least I know they're keeping Viktoria protected. The update Reaper texted me on my way over here said she was out of surgery and had lost a lot of blood, so it was touch and go, but she was fighting. The best news I could have hoped for in that regard and one less thing to worry about when I need to concentrate on getting Avery out of here.

The gunfire from upstairs stops as quickly as it started. "Hello, Mr. Riggs. I've been expecting you."

Christ. Perez sounds just like his brother.

"I would say I'm sorry about your brother, but I'm not. You'll be going to join him soon enough."

Perez issues a long, dark chuckle. "Many have tried to take us out in the past, and many have failed."

"I got your brother, didn't I? I decimated every one of your businesses. You have nothing left."

He releases a cold, sinister laugh. "Nothing left? You underestimate me. You have no idea the kind of reach our organization truly has. With my brother running our businesses in the West and in the South, that left me with our East Coast expansion, which had been going quite well until Avery and Amelia stumbled upon our little accounting error."

"You get off on hurting innocent women, Perez? Is that your thing?"

"You have me all wrong, Mr. Riggs. I am actually rather fond of Avery and hate having to do this to her, but she's left me no choice."

My hand tightens on my weapon, eager to put a bullet through this guy's head. "What about your wife or children, Perez? How would you feel if I told you I stopped by your house before I came here and did to them exactly what you did to Amelia?"

Silence greets me, but then a chuckle fills the stairwell. "I would tell you you're full of shit. I moved them out of town the moment *South of the Border* went up in flames. I saw another attack coming. I just never anticipated it would be from someone like you—"

"I'm not going to stop until I have Avery."

"Then come and try to get her."

I can almost see the smile in his statement. He thinks he has the upper hand, and while he does have the high ground, he doesn't have what I do—skills that make me lethal and an unbreakable will.

Nothing he can do will stop me from getting to Avery.

My heart thunders against my ribs as I toss a flashbang up the steps. It goes off; the sound is almost deafening, smoke filling the air. I move instantly, taking advantage of his disorientation.

His cough leads me straight to him, and I fire two shots in the direction of the sound as I race up through the smoke. I hit the top step, and something solid slams into me from the side, knocking me to the hallway floor.

Perez falls on top of me, his heavy weight keeping me prone, and he presses the barrel of his gun to my temple. He sneers at me, his eyes watering from the smoke. "I'm going to enjoy doing this up close and personal."

"So am I."

I pull the trigger on my pistol pinned between us. The bullet goes up into his chest, and his eyes widen, his body going limp almost instantly, gun tumbling from his hand next to my ear.

It was a calculated risk. Shooting him could have caused him to fire right into my head, but it wouldn't have mattered if I had died. As long as he's gone, Avery would be safe.

Avery...

She must be up here somewhere.

So close.

I grunt, struggling to push him off me with one fully functioning arm, and manage to roll him to one side. Blood pools from his chest and under him into beige carpeting. I grab the wall for support and push to my feet, kicking away his weapon even though he's never touching it again.

"Avery?"

Her name echoes through the hall, and I pause for a moment, both to listen for a response and to try to stop the world from tilting sideways.

I try to blink away the fuzziness from my vision and stumble down the hall toward the first bedroom.

Empty.

"Avery?"

One by one, I clear each room without any sign of her. My chest tightens with the possibility that she isn't here, or if she is, that I'm too late...

The master bedroom stands at the end of the hall, and a muffled noise from behind the closed door steals my breath. Weapon ready, I approach cautiously and turn the knob, pushing the door open.

Oh, God...

"Avery!"

AVERY

A FAMILIAR VOICE cuts through the gloom, something pulling at me, trying to drag me from the horrific place I've been.

Kalen?

I try to cry out to him, try to answer, but all that comes escapes is a muffled groan through my split lips. Pain drives at my temple where Ricardo struck me, relentless and agonizing.

Tears drop onto my legs, my head hanging limp from a neck that can't support it anymore. I manage to blink my eyes open, but I can't lift my head to see what's going on around me.

The door creaks open, and I squeeze my eyes closed and turn as much away as I can in case it's Ricardo again.

"Avery!"

Kalen's voice pulls me back toward the door, and familiar hands lift my face. Blood trickles from my split lip down my chin, and the blue eyes I've longed to swim in forever meet mine, dark with concern. I try to focus on his face, on the fact that he's right here, but everything is blurred, distant.

"That motherfucker! If he wasn't already dead, I would fucking kill him." He kneels in front of me, still holding my face between his hands, keeping my head up. "Are you okay?"

I attempt to move my arms and wince against the restraints still securing them behind my back. "I...he..."

"Fuck." Kalen gently releases my face and shifts behind me, pulling a knife from his boot. "I'm getting you out of here."

He cuts me free, and my hands fall limp at my sides. One of his strong arms wraps around me and pulls me toward the edge of the chair. "We have to get out of here before the cops show up."

"Cops?" I scan the room, trying to process his words. "What's going on?"

Kalen glances toward the hallway. "It's over. Perez is dead, and so are his men. But I've made a hell of a lot of noise doing it. We don't have much time."

I shake my head against the fog enveloping it, narrowing my eyes on the open doorway. "Okay, let's go."

Only my absolute will allows me to try to push up onto my feet, but my legs collapse under me.

Kalen's hold keeps me from face-planting the bloody floor. "I got you."

He grimaces and scoops me up into his arms, jaw locked. His skin pales, sweat beading on his forehead, and he wavers slightly on his feet. Viktoria's words float through my head...

Kalen's been shot.

"Kalen, are you okay?"

"I'm fine." He barely gets the words out between gritted teeth. "We have to move."

My eyes drift down to the bandage and tourniquet wrapped around his left bicep. "You can't carry me."

He shakes his head and locks eyes with me, the look he offers telling me the discussion is finished. "I'm fine. I got you."

The corner of my eye catches a flash of movement in the doorway, and a man steps forward.

"Kalen, watch out!"

Kalen whirls faster than I've ever seen anyone move, transferring me to my feet, blocking me with his body, and pulling the trigger on the gun in his right hand all at the same time.

Glass shatters across the room, and multiple bullets hit the man in the doorway square in the chest and right between the eyes. He collapses in a pile on the floor, and Kalen and I both whip our heads toward the broken window pane.

Without the benefit of any sunlight, I can't see anything beyond that. "Where did that come from?"

The tiniest smile graces Kalen's lips. "Mouth...I told him where I was heading, but I never expected him to come." He holds out his hand to me. "Can you walk?"

Even if I couldn't, I wouldn't tell him that now that

the fog is finally starting to clear and I can see how bad he truly is—pale, shaking, barely staying vertical.

Kalen takes a few steps toward the hallway, then stumbles, leaning against the wall for a second, sweat trickling down his almost-white skin. He slowly sags to his knees, using his shoulder to keep himself upright.

"Oh, God." I clamber over to him and slide my arm under his. "I got you, Kalen. Come on."

He tries to get his feet under him, putting almost all his weight on me, but even using all the energy left in my body, I can't get him upright. His body falls limply onto the floor, and I release a sob as tears stream down my face again.

I take his face in my hands and shake gently. "Kalen, wake up!" My tears fall onto him, but even that doesn't get him to budge. "Kalen, wake *up*. Please! We have to go!"

The thought of what will happen to him if the police show up makes me heave and stagger to my feet.

I have to get him out of here.

Pressing my hand against the wall to keep from falling over, my vision blurs from the tears and what is likely a wicked concussion. I make it a few steps down the hall before my foot hits something.

I look down into the open, dead eyes of Ricardo—a gaping wound in his chest, blood soaking the carpet under him.

All this death.

Because of *him*.

I turn my head to the side and empty the acid from my stomach as I force myself to keep moving.

Have to get help...

The throbbing in my head makes it almost impossible to focus, and I stumble again, the world spinning. I stare down the steps, and everything twists sideways, a wicked case of vertigo threatening to make me heave again.

I lower my foot to the first step, then stumble and slide down two or three more. A dark, hulking shadow appears at the bottom of the stairs, I blink rapidly to try to focus while I scramble up backward, but he's on me in two quick steps, dragging me upward with impossibly strong hands.

"No, please don't—"

A large, calloused palm cups my cheek and shakes my face gently, and I open my eyes to familiar ones.

"Mouth?" I throw my arms around his neck and hold him tightly, a cry slipping from my lips. "Kalen's up there. He won't wake up."

Mouth nods his understanding, then rushes down the steps and carries me onto the front lawn. A black SUV sits running at the curb, and he opens the back door and lowers me into it.

Before I can ask him anything, he double-times it back into the house. Waiting for him to return with Kalen is sheer agony, like more knives being shoved into my heart with each passing second.

Seeing his massive frame in the door with Kalen over his shoulder finally allows me to release a heavy, relieved breath. He runs across the yard, dumps Kalen into the backseat with me, and slams the door.

"Kalen?" I scramble across the backseat to him, running my hands over his face. "Mouth, how long ago was he shot?"

Mouth glances at me in the rearview mirror as we peel away from the curb but doesn't say anything; he just drives like a bat out of hell away from the quiet, suburban neighborhood that's now been wracked by more gunshots than they've probably ever heard before.

We barrel toward the highway, but rather than feeling relieved to be free of Perez's threat, a new fear grips me, staring down at Kalen and his blood-soaked arm.

"Is Kalen going to be okay?"

The big, silent man offers me a hard stare in the rearview mirror but doesn't answer, either because he doesn't know or because he doesn't want me to know the truth.

17

CHAOS

The door to the bedroom of Reaper's guest room where I've been laid up opens slowly, and Avery slips inside, turning to try to quietly ease it shut without waking me.

"I'm up."

She jumps and whirls toward me, her hand pressed over her chest. "Jesus, you scared the crap out of me."

Shit.

"I'm sorry. I didn't mean to."

The last few days haven't helped ease her constant fear. Even knowing Perez is gone and most of his organization decimated, she's always on edge, always anticipating the worst and reacting to even the smallest things with a racing heart, tears, or a full-blown meltdown.

Who can blame her?

She's been to Hell and back, but she came out alive. I keep trying to remind her of that while also reminding myself that she doesn't have the benefit of having seen as much as I have. It doesn't affect me the way it does her but being so close to losing her has left me nervous every time she leaves the room, which is why I didn't sleep a wink while she was visiting Viktoria with Reaper.

We have eyes on Perez's henchman still operating in other regions of the country, but they won't be a problem. With as many friends as we have, they'll be taken out one by one before they can stir up any shit.

She examines me with a keen eye, looking for signs of how I'm feeling because she knows I'll never complain or admit how weak or in pain I really am. "Did you talk to Preacher?"

I nod. "Yep, he's confident he scrubbed any traces of what we did from any security cameras, and he's continuing to monitor Baltimore PD for anything that spells trouble for us. We'll still need to come up with a solid story for you to give the cops since we know they're looking for you to talk about what happened at the diner. But right now, it appears they're focused on rival cartels as the perpetrators, especially due to the almost simultaneous attack on their compound in Mexico. We just need to wait until all your bruises heal for you to go get things tied up with them and with Bernice."

"So, you and the guys are in the clear?"

"We're in the clear." I push myself up with my good

arm, struggling to bite back a groan at the ache still overtaking my body. Waiting to get my wound properly treated left me fighting both blood loss and a nasty infection and knocked me the fuck out for days. Other than lying in bed and having Mouth and Avery take care of me, I haven't been able to do much else. "How's Viktoria today?"

Avery makes her way across the room to me and lowers herself to the mattress next to me as I wince and sit up with my back against the headboard. She watches me try to hide my pain but bites back her usual comment about it. "Better. Ready to get out of the damn hospital and being very vocal about it, but the doctor said probably another week before she can go home."

I snort and shake my head. "That doesn't surprise me at all. Vik isn't the type who enjoys being laid up."

Her green eyes flash with humor, and the corner of her almost-healed lips twitches. "Reminds me of someone else I know."

"Let's not argue about that again." I brush my fingers along her exposed arm. "I'm tired of that conversation."

She narrows her gaze on me. "You think that was arguing?"

"Wasn't it?"

I'm not sure I can take another disagreement over how I should be staying in bed or how I'm overdoing it after almost dying from blood loss and shock only a few days ago just by showering or using the damn bathroom.

Avery grins at me. "You've been single for too long. You don't remember what an argument really is."

I grin at her. "We never argued."

Something flashes deep in her eyes, a pain I hadn't expected to see while we're just joking around, and she throws her head. "No, we didn't. We just fucked like you hated me once you stopped loving me."

Her words make me stiffen, and I shift uncomfortably against the headboard, though not from the pain still lingering in my arm but because of how insane her words truly are. "That's what you think? That I didn't love you? That *that* was why I was acting the way I was...because I was attracted to you but didn't *love* you?"

Even saying the words is enough to make me fist my hands at my sides to fight the desire to destroy something.

Avery examines me, her mouth opening and closing a few times. "I-I guess. What else was I supposed to think? All you ever did was fuck me, and then you would leave as if you couldn't bear to be around me."

"Jesus, Avery..." I drag her to me, clutching her against my chest and pulling her face between my palms firmly, ensuring she's looking me in the eyes and can see my sincerity as I say these words to her. "How could you possibly believe that?" I swallow back the emotion threatening to choke me. "I didn't leave you because I didn't love you, Avery. I left *because* I loved you more than anything. Because I was trying to protect you. I was trying to keep you safe, just like I am now."

Her lips quiver, and tears pool in her eyes. "Protect me from what?"

"From *me*. From what I might have done to you."

"What you might have done to me? I don't..." She shakes her head again, tears streaming down her cheeks. "I don't understand what you're saying."

This is a conversation I never wanted to have with her, one I've avoided for half a damn decade, but after everything that's happened between us, I owe her an explanation. She needs to understand why it's not safe for us to be together, why we *can't* go back to how it was before.

I take a deep breath, fighting with the words I've kept buried deep inside me for so long. "After I came back from that mission, when I was in the hospital, I started having nightmares. Horrifying and violent ones about some of the things that happened. That's why I never wanted you around, never wanted you to spend the night there. Every time I fell asleep, it would happen, and it was always worse at night."

The memories of those nights, of the terror and panic that seized me, tighten my gut, but I have to tell her. I have to get this out, so she'll truly understand why it isn't safe to be with me.

"One night...when one of the nurses came in to check on me...I almost killed her."

Avery's eyes widen. "What?"

"I woke up with two nurses trying to get my hands off the neck of this woman. I was choking her, Avery. I was literally strangling the life out of that woman because I couldn't see her. I couldn't understand what was happening around me. I was so lost in my own head, in my dream and my memories, that I didn't know what I was doing. And I almost killed her. If she hadn't been able to reach over and hit the emergency button next to the bed, I don't..." I shake my head and squeeze my eyes closed. "I can't even think about what might have happened."

"Oh, my God, Kalen." A soft hand brushes my cheek. "Why didn't they tell me? Why didn't *you* tell me?"

I tighten my grip on her face, needing her to understand. "Because I didn't want you to see me like that. I didn't want you to be afraid of me. Someone higher up ran interference with the woman I hurt and the hospital to ensure I wasn't going to get charged or punished for what happened. At that point in time, they were concerned about getting me back in the unit. They didn't want anything to interfere with that. Not you. Not some lawsuit from the nurse I fucked up while *I* was fucked up."

I pull my hands off her face, talking about what I did suddenly making me fear touching her right now.

You can't hurt her any more than you already have.

"I couldn't trust myself with you anymore, Avery. I couldn't trust what I would do if I slept next to you, if I held you in my arms, even when that's the only thing that ever felt right. The only time I ever felt normal after what happened."

"Kalen..." Her lips tremble, and she swipes at her tears. "You could have told me. You *should* have told me. I thought—"

"I thought I knew what I was doing. I thought I was protecting you, but I was also too selfish to fully give you up. Because I loved you. I *still* love you. And the only time I felt *okay* was when we were together, even if it was just for sex." I struggle to come up with words to explain everything that happened back then, for the way I suffer every day. "When I deployed again, I had hoped being there with the guys, getting back to work, would...I don't know, maybe snap me out of it and I could come back, and I could be everything I used to be for you. But—"

"But instead, you came back...and I had already moved out of the house and served you divorce papers."

The worst fucking day of my life.

Being given those papers felt like holding my entire life in my hand and watching it burn. That day I signed them, it felt like I had died, and I haven't really been living since then.

I nod slowly. "Yeah. And I couldn't blame you. Not really. After how I acted, after what I did to you. You had every right to divorce me and to believe what you did. I'm just so sorry it made you feel like you weren't enough for me."

"No." She shakes her head, reaching out to clutch at my chest. "*I* am. I should have pushed you harder to talk to me. I should have forced you to tell me what was going on. Maybe if I had—"

"No." I lean forward and silence her with a finger over her lips. "You can't blame yourself for any of this. I won't let you. This is one hundred percent on me. *I'm* the only one who made mistakes here."

Avery squeezes her eyes closed, refusing to look at me. "That's not true."

"What do you mean?"

"I made so many mistakes, Kalen. So many damn mistakes."

"What are you talking about?"

"No matter what you say, I should have tried harder. I should have pushed. I should have known that you loved me and that whatever was happening to us was something else. But I was an emotional mess, especially toward the end when I talked to the attorney and got the divorce papers."

She opens her eyes. The pain there is so deep, so real that I can physically feel it weighing down on top of my own.

"I was pregnant."

I freeze, ice flooding through my veins. "You were what?"

"It must have happened right before you left again. You were gone for about two months, and we left things on such bad terms that I didn't want to tell you while you were over there. We barely spoke as it was, and I didn't want you to have that weighing on you on top of everything else for your first mission back." Her tears fall in earnest now, mixing with the sobs she can't fight back. "I was going to tell you the next time we saw each other, when we had to sign the papers, but..."

"But what?"

"I had a miscarriage before we had the meeting. The baby was just...gone. I felt like maybe it was a sign that we were doing the right thing. It erased any doubts I still had lingering about signing those papers."

"And you never told me..."

She chokes on a sob, pressing her hand over her mouth. "And I never told you that you were going to be a father. Instead, I went into that meeting angry and took it out on you with the horrible things I said. I'm so sorry. I should have told you the truth."

Fear lives in her gaze as she stares back at me—for how I'm going to react to this news, for how I might lash out. She's expecting me to be mad at her, to be furious about the fact that she kept something so important from me.

But she couldn't be more wrong.

My heart shatters, thinking about what she went through, what she had to endure completely on her own. I was all she had, and I pushed her away, isolated myself from her, therefore isolating *her* from the only person she could ever rely on it.

"You went through that all by yourself..." Guilt cuts at me, more painful than any time I've been shot. "I'm so sorry. I should have been here with you. We should have been together, supporting each other. We wouldn't be sitting here like this if I had been."

"But we *are* here." Avery offers a sad smile, one I've seen far too much in the last few days since I rescued her from Perez. "This is our reality now, where we are."

I pull her hand into mine and squeeze it. "The truth is, I still have those nightmares. I wake up in a cold sweat and can't always come back to reality right away. It's why I don't sleep. I try to avoid it."

"That's why you left the bedroom the other night, why you wouldn't sleep with me while I was here."

I nod slowly. "I knew it would be safer for you if I didn't stay." The words I don't want to say sit on my tongue like lead weights. "Nothing has changed, Avery. I love you more than anything, which is why I'll never let you be in danger around me."

AVERY

I LOVE you more than anything...but we can't be together.

That's what he's saying without *really* saying it. He can't even form the words because he knows it's wrong.

We finally came clean with each other. After *everything* that happened, we're finally in a position to make things right, to have a second chance at what we failed so miserably at once before. But he's pushing me away, trying to send me back to that lonely, horrible life I had without him.

I lean in, lowering my forehead against his. Our breaths mingle, my body coming awake again this close to him after so many days, avoiding touching him for fear I would hurt him. But he seems stronger today, strong enough to finally tell me the truth, to open the door for me to tell him what I've kept locked away for so long.

And he loves me

Hearing those words from him almost made everything I've suffered worth it. It was the one thing I thought I had lost and could never get back, but really, I had it all along. Viktoria was right about that—about a lot of things, actually. And now Kalen is trying to destroy what we've finally found again because he's scared.

I'm scared, too. Absolutely terrified that this is all some dream I'll wake up from to find him gone again. But I won't let him run away again. He won't shut me out.

I ghost my lips over his softly. "It's not the same as before, Kalen. Everything has changed now. I know the truth, and I'm not going to let you push me away this time. I refuse to give up on you and me."

His heart thunders under my palm, and I curl my fingers into his warm flesh, needing to feel him, all of him, so he can't find a way to put up another wall between us again.

"This, you and me, Kalen, it was always meant to be forever. We just got in the fucking way."

We're older now—battered and bruised and scarred by life and the horrible things in it. But also wiser. We know better. We're stronger. We're finally being honest with each other for the first time, and that means *everything*.

He considers me for a minute, our bodies pressed together, my hand pinned between us. "Do you really believe that?"

"I always have." I shake my head, running my free hand back through his unruly hair. "We both have been miserable for years. Neither one of us getting what we wanted out of this divorce. So why? Why do we keep doing this to ourselves? Whatever is going on with you...we can figure it out. *Together*."

"That's what you want?"

I nod and kiss him again. "That's what I want. That's what I need. You. Us together like this."

He inhales deeply and swallows slowly. "You know what the guys and I do, right? What our business is?" Concern furrows his brow. "Do you really understand who I am?"

Who he is?

That question pulls at something deep inside me, something I've known since I met him. I stare into his blue eyes, the ones I've loved since I was sixteen. "I have always known *exactly* who you are, Kalen Riggs. I've always known there was something chaotic deep inside you. It's what drew me to you in the first place.

You are always so fearless. It was exciting, addictive. And I always knew what you did. Maybe not the details. But I knew enough. I knew who you had to become to do that job and then come back to me and pretend like you didn't. I know you tried to separate yourself from Chaos. But I always knew who he was. And I've loved Kalen *and* Chaos the entire time."

Tears roll from his eyes, and it isn't because the pain medication is likely wearing off. He didn't even cry when we got married, so to see this now both gives me hope and makes me fear that he may do exactly what he's so used to doing—push me away.

If I lose Kalen again, I don't know that I'd survive it.

Murder. Kidnapping. Beatings. All of *that* would be nothing compared to what I would suffer knowing he walked away again.

"You really mean that, Avery?"

"I don't care what other people might think about what you're doing. I know you, and I know those boys out there. None of you would do it if you didn't think the people you were doing it to deserve it one hundred percent. I believe in what you guys are trying to accomplish, and I don't need to know the specifics." I lower my forehead to his again, tangling my fingers in the hair at his nape. "I trust you. I trust Reaper and Mouth and Viktoria, and I trust Chaos."

Kalen's stillness and silence makes a vise tighten around my chest, and I pull back slightly. He raises his hand and drags me back to him, brushing his lips over mine.

"I never thought I'd hear you say that. I never thought I would have another chance with you again." He kisses me deeply, dragging me fully on top of him. "Christ, I love you, woman."

I try to back off from his prone body. "Stop, Kalen. You're going to hurt yourself."

He grins at me, the light I haven't seen in years finally touching his eyes again like it used to. "I don't care."

Maybe I don't, either.

My body heats at his touch, seeking what I always have from him—comfort, passion, acceptance, love.

He pulls me back down onto him, gliding his tongue along mine, his hands finding my ass and positioning me across his lap to grind me against his hardening cock. "I'm so sorry it took us this long to figure it out, babe."

"But we did. We figured it the fuck out, and we'll figure out anything else we need to in the future."

The future.

Something I thought we could never have, something I thought *I* might not have when I made that call to Kalen, seeking help. There were so many times it was almost snatched away from us, almost stolen not only by evil men with evil intent but also by ourselves being stupid and stubborn.

Never again.

"Together. We'll figure it out together."

He grins at me. "Right."

This man has always known exactly how to take

care of me, how to make me feel everything exactly as I should. This moment is no different. He groans into my mouth, dragging me impossibly closer against him, demanding what we both want.

The fingers of his left hand tighten on my hip as his right slips over my thigh and between my legs to rub in exactly the right spot. I moan against his lips, grinding against him, even though I should probably climb off and let him rest.

The last thing we should be doing is *this* right now, but after almost dying, after watching him fight for his life after saving mine, we both need something life-affirming, something that *feels* good, something that is for *us*.

"Kalen..."

He answers my plea by taking my mouth in a desperate kiss, rolling his hips to mine. Any pain or exhaustion that has kept him down the last few days disappears in a single second, both of us needing this more than we need to acknowledge any potential restrictions.

I push down his boxers, freeing his cock, which strains toward me. Taking it in my hand, I stroke him slowly, brushing the pad of my thumb across the head. He groans and thrusts into my grip, and my pussy clenches, seeking what's so close.

His frantic hands shove at the waistband of my yoga pants, pushing them and my thong down my thighs, and I release him long enough to slide them off and toss them onto the floor.

Kalen's heated gaze rakes over me, and he takes his cock in his hand and strokes it languidly, watching as I pull my shirt up and off. His eyes drop to my breasts, and I climb across the mattress and straddle him again.

He reaches out and captures my breasts in his rough palms, flicking his thumb across the nipples and sending tiny jolts of pleasure straight to my clit. I groan and grasp his cock, gliding it through the wetness already pooling between my legs. His mouth finds mine again, hungry and determined, and I align him with my pussy and sink down onto his cock, his flesh spreading me wide open, filling me and the place that's always belonged to him.

My mouth falls open on a gasp that he swallows down, stroking my tongue with his as his hands find my hips and squeeze, urging me to move. I lean back and raise myself up, locking my gaze with his so I can watch his blue eyes darken as I slowly engulf his cock again and again.

His fingers dig into my skin, hard enough to leave bruises, but I don't care how he marks me. He already owns me, all of me. It doesn't matter whether he's Kalen or Chaos; he will always have me and my heart.

Whether he likes it or not.

He can fight me, fight this, try to push me away again, but I won't let him. Whatever happens in our future, we'll face it together.

I roll my hips and set a slow rhythm that he matches with his thrusts up. We move together fluidly, like waves crashing against the shore, like we were always meant to be like this. Because we were. We *are*.

We were just too wrapped up in our own pain to see it and accept it.

It may have taken both of us almost dying to finally find each other, but now that we have, I'll do anything to ensure I never lose him again.

I squeeze his cock, watching the muscles in his neck and jaw tighten, and he slides a hand down until his thumb finds my clit. My hips jerk at the contact, and he sits up to take one of my nipples into his mouth, sucking and flicking it with his tongue while I grind on him, feeding the slow warmth building between my legs.

He moves to my other breast, giving it the same treatment. I gasp and drop my head down to bite into the flesh of his shoulder, my pace increasing as he braces his feet on the mattress and thrusts up, driving himself even deeper.

"Fucking hell." Kalen issues a low growl as I sweep my tongue across the mark I just made on his body. "Come for me, Avery. Come for me and then marry me again."

"Wait...what?" I return my focus to him, blinking away what must be enough lust to completely fog my brain. "What did you just—"

"Marry me. Again." He captures my face in his hand and grips me tightly, bringing my lips to his. "The biggest mistake I ever made in my life was walking away from you. I got so off course that I never thought I could get back on it. But now that we are, I don't ever want to lose you again. So, marry me."

It was the last thing I expected him to say, but there is only one possible answer.

"*Yes*."

Mrs. Kalen "Chaos" Riggs...

It has a nice ring to it.

Want more from these badass former military men? Grab *Clean Slate*, Mouth's story and the third book in the Scarred Heroes Series.
Books2read.com/CleanSlateGM

Want more from the Sins of the Mafia World?

Grab the Sins of the Mafia Collections here: https://books2read.com/rl/SinsoftheMafiaWorld

Sign up for Gwyn's newsletter to stay up to date on releases and other news: www.gwynmcnamee.com/newsletter

ABOUT THE AUTHOR

Gwyn McNamee is an attorney, writer, wife, and mother (to one human baby and two fur babies). Originally from the Midwest, Gwyn relocated to her husband's home town of Las Vegas in 2015 and is enjoying her respite from the cold and snow. Gwyn has been writing down her crazy stories and ideas for years and finally decided to share them with the world. She loves to write stories with a bit of suspense and action mingled with romance and heat.

When she isn't either writing or voraciously devouring any books she can get her hands on, Gwyn is busy adding to her tattoo collection, golfing, and stirring up trouble with her perfect mix of sweetness and sarcasm (usually while wearing heels).

Gwyn loves to hear from her readers.
Here is where you can find her:
NewsletteR:
www.gwynmcnamee.com/newsletter
Facebook:
https://www.facebook.com/AuthorGwynMcNamee/
Twitter:
https://twitter.com/GwynMcNamee